SÉAMUS O'FLYNN

New York Diaries of An Immigrant Son 1931-1945

Bill Tobin

Printed in the United States of America.

ISBN-10: 1456308971
EAN-13: 9781456308971

For information, contact the author at:
email: billtobin21@comcast.net
web site: billtobinbook.com

"Séamus O'Flynn" can be purchased in paperback or downloaded to an e-book reader at amazon.com/books

Special thanks to Rita Sweetnam
for her father's poem "The Brave I.R.A."

To my inspirational immigrant parents, Patrick & Kathleen.
To Anne, for 50 years of consummate love;
Our children: Caroline, Guy, Paul, Jen.
My siblings: Kitty, Patsy, Mary Rita, Peter, Gail

ONE

While the gray clouds of the Great Depression continued darkening, two awesome events occurred during 1931 in New York City. On May first, President Herbert Hoover pressed a magic button in the White House switching on lights two hundred miles away in the new Empire State Building; on October twenty-fifth the first automobile crossed the new George Washington Bridge connecting New York and New Jersey.

On December 9th I was born in a Hell's Kitchen clinic.

In the midst of a collapsing economy and expanding bread lines, the completion of the world's tallest skyscraper and longest suspension bridge gave reasons to celebrate. After my christening at St Luke's Church in the South Bronx my parents took my sister Siohban, two, and me to the top of the Empire State, followed by a blustery evening stroll over the George Washington Bridge.

My mother says of course the Great Depression was painful for them, but they never lost hope. My father says Irish immigrants like my parents adapted quickly to life in America because they brought with them, besides a lone suitcase, their Catholic faith that had toughened them, given them hope during hundreds of years of suffering and starvation under the British.

MY EARLIEST MEMORY - *ice cream.*

I'm four, sitting with my mother and six year old sister Siohban in the back of a Yellow cab, devouring a chocolate ice cream cone. It's my first time in a car and first time in a taxi. My sister and I have just had our tonsils out at Flower Fifth Avenue Hospital in Manhattan and we're coming home to our apartment at 680 East 139th Street. This is the happiest day of my life. I am cruising in a taxi up Fifth Avenue, over the Harlem River into the Bronx. My throat is sore but the cold chocolate soothes the pain.

My second memory is an inebriated five-year-old.

The ad in the *New York Times* read: *"FOR RENT, Four Rooms, $48 a month. In the beautiful residential section off Fordham Road in the suburban atmosphere of University Heights, North of N.Y.U. Bronx Campus. Around the corner from St Nicholas Catholic School."*

"We're moving to Fordham Road. We're moving *Up Town*," my mother says turning her Irish brogue into a fake English accent. She means the O'Flynns are migrating a few miles from the South Bronx to the North Bronx.

My parents are packing everything in boxes. I spot some red soda in a strange tall bottle. It doesn't smell like Pepsi Cola. I hide inside the hall closet and take a sip. Bitter. But I'm thirsty.

"Have you seen Séamus?" my mother asks my younger sister Sinead.

"He's hiding," Sinead says.

"I saw him with a coke," Siohban says.

I've drained half the bottle. I'm not feeling good. Now I'm throwing up macaroni in the closet. Moaning.

"I hear him," my father says.

I fall against the closet door and spill out onto the floor, dregs of the Dubonnet wine dripping down my shirt.

"Lord Preserve Us. He's dead," my mother screams.

"No he isn't," my father says. "He's got the *jim-jams*."

My father tells my mother to hold my arms behind my back. He sticks his finger down my throat and I heave more pink macaroni.

"Let's rush him to the hospital," my mother says.

"Calm down, Kit. He'll be fine. His legs are a bit rubbery, that's all."

In my uncle Jim's open truck I'm stretched out on a mattress, one Bayer aspirin in my stomach, my father comforting me on the bumpy ride along the Grand Concourse. My mother and sisters are in the front of the truck with Uncle Jim. I hear my mother say: "What will our new neighbors think when they see us moving in with a tipsy five year old?"

The truck makes a left turn off the Grand Concourse onto Fordham Road. Good. My new neighborhood has many more movie theaters and candy stores.

"There's St Nick's and your new school," my mother yells. One block from the massive cathedral-like church we make a left turn up a steep hill. The truck pulls up in front of 222 Loring Place, a five-storied, redbrick apartment building.

My distress from the Dubonnet wine is fading. The wind blowing on my face in the back of the open truck on this humid August afternoon helps clear my head. My father has a bath towel ready should additional macaroni wish to escape my queasy stomach. "You've never seen me tipsy," my father chuckles, "but I've already seen my soon-to-be-first-grader crashing out of a closet."

MY FATHER RUNS up the stairs two at a time to the fourth floor. I walk behind my mother and sisters worrying there won't be a bedroom for me. The superintendent opens the door to 4C and my father points out the bathroom near the front door. Next is the bedroom for Sinead and Siobhan. They express delight at their spacious room. Over here my father says is our bedroom. I see the fire escape and I'm glad this isn't my room. We continue down the long hall. I'm looking for another doorway. My father enters the living room.

"You'll have the open-out couch here," my father says sheepishly.

"I still have to sleep in the living room?" I plead.

"We can't afford a third bedroom," he says.

"But I've never had a room of my own," I protest. "Put Sinead and Siobhan in the living room this time and give me the bedroom."

"That wouldn't be fair," my mother says. "There are two of them, and only one of you. You can hang your clothes in the hall closet over there. You'll see, you'll be comfortable."

It isn't comfort I'm looking for. I don't like the dark. I don't like pulling my bed out of a couch every night. I dread bedtime. The radio is turned off at nine-thirty and my sisters say goodnight. With my bed open I'm surrounded on all sides by large pieces of furniture. I lie on my stomach and feel both sides of my body twinge. An arm of a chair is going to reach out and touch me.

My mother helps me pull my bed out and kisses me when I get in.

I tell her I'm concerned someone might come in the living room window from the fire escape.

"No one will get you," she assures me. "Why would they want you? All kidnapped children are rich. Kidnappers want ransom money. The only thing of value in this apartment is my engagement ring."

"Frankenstein picked up a child," I say.

"But there's no Frankenstein, Séamus. No King Kong or Dracula. Someone made up the stories that were made into movies. I warned you. You should stop seeing such frightening movies. Now, say your prayers."

When my mother turns off the light, I close my eyes and say one Our Father, one Hail Mary and Now I Lay Me Down to Sleep.

"...and if I die before I wake...." I don't want to die in the middle of the night. If I do it's because someone will climb up the fire escape and come in that window over there. I'm not going to say that prayer anymore. I think I'll just concentrate on the Our Father and Hail Mary. Reciting prayers and keeping my eyes shut tight does calm me down. I know God will protect me. And my Guardian Angel is stretched out next to me in this open-out-couch. But I still check the lock on the window.

TWO

In the fall we have goose for dinner so my mother can drain off her winter supply of medicinal fat. She stores large jars of goose fat in the icebox.

Mrs Mendelsson in 1C, the only Jews in 222, swears her chicken soup is the best way to stem a cold. My mother swears by Lux Flakes and goose fat.

I cough into my pillow at night so my mother can't hear me.

"Do I hear bronchitis coming on?" she asks.

"No. Just a slight cough," I say.

When she takes the box of Lux Flakes from the cupboard I know the only way I can avoid her healing crusade is to run away from home.

She dissolves the soap flakes in lukewarm water ("Only Lux has these exquisite tissue-thin flakes" she assures me), pours the mixture into a big red rubber bag and hangs it on the shower curtain rod.

"Oh no," I protest. "It's only a slight cough, mom." But there's no place to hide in our cramped apartment. I drop my pants and stretch face down on a pile of soft towels on the bathroom floor.

"A little dab of Vaseline and we're ready," she says kissing the back of my head as the tip of the tube enters. "It will only hurt for a moment or so." I hear the metal clamp snap open and feel the hot liquid going inside. "The more you hold, the faster you'll be better."

"I'm starting to get cramps," I yell.

"Just a little more, Séamus," she says squeezing the bag. I wish Mrs Mendelsson were my mother.

I have no idea where the Lux liquid is going. How can a whole bag of warm water fit inside me? My mother says soap washes dirt off your hands, out of clothes. Same scientific principle, and there's no harmful alkali she says. All those cold germs stuck to your insides are being washed off right now, ready to come out.

"That's it mom. No more."

"Hold tight, Séamus."

"That's it, *really*."

"Hop on the toilet. I'll be back in a few minutes."

Part two of my mother's cure is the rub down with warm goose fat on my chest and back.

"The germs have been flushed away," my mother explains in a soft voice. "Now this warm fat goes deep into your pores and draws out the rest of the cold germs hiding in your skin. They haven't got a chance. It works just like a hot poultice that draws pus out of a boil. This soothing unction penetrates your lungs and softens your bronchitis." My mother's finishing touch is to entirely wrap my chest with strips of old bed sheets. I look like the mummies I see at the Metropolitan Museum of Art.

"O.K., now it's your turn Siobhan," my mother says to my sister picking up the box of Lux again.

Every Sunday night our family listens to the radio. My sisters and I lay on the living room floor with pillows under our heads. We stare into the ceiling where we can almost see what's happening. Jack Benny at seven, George Burns and Gracie Allen, followed by the *Lux Radio Theater*. When the announcer says, "Welcome to *Lux Radio Theater*" my sisters and I shudder. "Lux is safe for anything that's safe in water. Fine lingerie deserves fine care. New quick Lux is mild and gentle. It suds fast, too. And a little goes so far, it's thrifty."

"Listen children," my father says. "He says Lux adds life to your underwear. Just think what it does when it's washing your insides."

OUR FAMILY DOCTOR is Uncle Cronan McCaffrey whose office is in his home in Bayonne, New Jersey. His parents emigrated to America in the late eighteen hundreds and in 1934 Cronan became the first doctor in the O'Flynn-O'Leary families. In his last year of medical school, Cronan spotted my aunt Fanny at a Corkmen's Dance. She's the beauty of the O'Leary family. A doctor is a great catch my mother says.

For our free yearly check-up we embark on a five-hour round trip from Loring Place to Main Street, Bayonne. All our O'Flynn relatives live in apartments in the Bronx, Upper Manhattan and Queens. I'm happy to go to Bayonne. Not for the doctor's exam, but to visit a grand home. My father calls it McCaffrey's Mahogany Mansion. He says they live the *Life of Reilly.* They live every greenhorn's dream. A house, a car, a cabin at Lake Mohawk. They don't live pay check to pay check my father says.

"But their family has been in the states for two generations," my mother points out.

My cousins have their own rooms, huge beds, dressers, chairs, drapes and bathrooms everywhere with tubs and separate stall showers. Luxury I see only in movies.

Our family arrives at six p.m. when Doctor McCaffrey is with his last patient. He's short, rotund, bald, meticulously dressed in a starched white shirt, silk tie with a small tight knot, black pants with a gray chalk stripe, mirror polished black shoes. A white jacket completes his professional look. I think he looks like an undertaker or a groom on his wedding day. My parents refer to Doctor McCaffrey in hushed tones. He's revered more than any priest or nun.

"This is serious," my father admonishes. "No giggling or scowling. He's more than an ordinary doctor. He's a heart specialist."

We sit on the bench outside his office. We're summoned one by one.

"Come in, Séamus," he says patting me on the back.

His stethoscope moves across my chest, stops at a few spots I figure are above my heart and then listens to whatever is under my back. A pencil light searches my eyes, ears and throat. He puts a drop of blood from my thumb onto a strip of cotton gauze and then slides it into a slot to compare with drops ranging from very pale pink to deep red. He stops when my blood color matches one of the circles. *"Huuummm,"* he chants. "See that red drop on the right Séamus. That's someone with healthy blood. Note your blood drop is somewhat lighter. That means you're anemic."

"Ahh-knee-mick," I stammer staring at my pale drop of blood. Those damned enemas have washed out my blood too.

"Nothing serious, Séamus," Doctor McCaffrey assures me. "Iron deficiency."

"Lux Flakes," I murmur.

"Fill these two prescriptions," he instructs my mother. "Low serum iron concentration. Two tablespoons of cod liver oil and two ounces of bottled beef blood every day. For breakfast, two raw eggs beaten into a glass of milk. You can add some Bosco or a dash of vanilla. With this regimen his anemia will be gone in a few months."

On the way back to New York I realize my continued well being now depends on oil from the livers of cod fish, soap flakes made from animal fat, blood from a heifer, fat from a goose and raw eggs from chickens. I wonder what else I'll be taking if I *really* get sick?

THREE

Halfway through Lent, my mother announces it's time for me to have a new suit. Living room furniture is tattered, carpets are threadbare, but my mother's priority is dressing my sisters and me like royalty. Everyone at St Nick's has splendid clothing for Sunday mass. At communion you come up the center aisle and process back down the side aisles. Heads piously bowed in prayer begin craning and spinning to check the latest University Heights' fashions. Women's hats get the most attention. At Easter my mother won't wear last year's hat. Nor could we be seen in year-old clothes.

"We're going to *Jewtown* on Saturday," my mother tells me. I wish I could wear last year's suit even though it's tight across my chest. I don't like going to the garment district off Canal Street. My Irish-Catholic, church-going, novena-pious, rosary-praying mother proudly boasts she can "*Jew* anyone down."

The worst part of the trip is getting on the subway. Change booth attendants don't complain if children pass under the turnstile without paying. When I was six I had to bend my neck to get under. But now I'm a full head above the turnstile.

Even though I don't ask, she feels obliged to explain why she isn't paying for me on the subway. "Under your father's *liberation* policy, we're not really stealing. We are not stealing a loaf of Wonder Bread from Safeway. *Nothing* is moving from one place to another. Mayor LaGuardia is not going to miss an O'Flynn nickel. It's just a ride on the subway. The train is going downtown whether we're on it or not." She tells me emphatically it's not a matter for confession.

At the Fordham Road IRT elevated station we wait at the top of the stairs while my mother reconnoiters. She waits until she can hear the clatter of the oncoming train. People start running up the stairs. Others, half a block away, break into a gallop. If you don't have a nickel you go to the change-booth. Change attendants have battle training for moments like this. Everyone is agitated. No one wants to wait fifteen minutes if they miss this train. If someone takes time to ask the attendant for directions, people on the line groan. This state of pandemonium is my mother's call to action. She waves her purse at me. Her signal to start running as fast as we can. She drops in a nickel and pushes my head down so I can get through the turnstile. On the subway, out of breath, she continues listing reasons for her subway subterfuge. "Your father's constantly reminding us of our sorry finances. During the early years of the Depression we didn't have one extra penny to buy *The Daily Mirror*. We just read the headlines on newsstands or listened to the radio."

My mother starts outlining her *Jewing-down* strategy as the subway passes Yankee Stadium heading toward the tunnel connecting the Bronx to Manhattan Island. When she says the suit I'm trying on is too expensive, I must go back into the dressing room and take it off. Put on your clothes again and come out with your eyes down. You must look forlorn. I'm not sure I know how to look forlorn.

Through the years my mother narrows the Canal Street suit-buying to Rabinovich's Men's Clothing and Finestein's Fine Apparel. The stores are directly across from each other. My mother recognizes Rabinovich and Finestein. They never seem to remember her. This makes me think the game about to be played is an everyday occurrence. It's not just a sport between Catholic and Jew.

Both stores sell almost the same clothing. But only one is going to get the O'Flynn sale. When Finestein sees us coming out of Rabinovichs he knows a bargain hasn't been struck. My mother knows Finestein is now more willing to cut into his profit. She realizes all shopkeepers in this neighborhood eagerly anticipate this opportunity to sell Catholics their annual Easter clothes. They won't be back at Christmas. One suit per year while you are growing. They won't let you get away without a sale.

"I'm looking for a suit for my son," she begins thickening her brogue. "Inexpensive, but good material."

Finestein begins: "Let's see. He must be a size thirty-two. This suit is one hundred percent worsted wool. Run your hand over the goods. It will wear like iron. Why don't you try it on, sonny?"

"And the price?" my mother demands.

"The price is not important. Let's see how the suit looks on him. What's your name, sonny?"

"Séamus," I say, wishing I were back on the IRT.

"Put this on, Séamus."

When I come out my mother asks if I like the suit. I nod yes.

"Go out in the street," Finestein says. "See the true color in the daylight. I'm not worried you'll run away. Ha. Ha. Ha. I trust you."

In front of the store my mother spots Rabinovich peeking out his display window. "If this doesn't work out Séamus, we'll go to Rabinovichs," my mother whispers. "The tag says twenty-three ninety-five. They put the price up twenty percent knowing they're going to get into a sparring match. It fits well, don't you think, Séamus?"

"Yes."

She opens her purse and takes out her wallet. She pulls out a few bills carefully counting them with a long face, hoping Finestein is paying attention.

"For Séamus it's twenty-one ninety-five," Finestein begins bargaining.

"A fair price would be sixteen dollars even," my mother says.

"At sixteen I don't have a profit. Sorry, no deal."

"We're leaving, Séamus. Take off the suit." She rolls her eyes in the direction of Rabinovichs and smiles at me so Finestein can see.

I go back to the dressing room and put on my clothes. There isn't a sound in the store. Finestein puts the suit back on the hanger. When I come out he holds the suit up to me and says my sandy hair and coloring are perfect with this shade of charcoal gray.

My mother walks slowly to the front door. "Let's go Séamus," she says, knowing she's about to win the battle.

"Nineteen ninety-five," says Finestein. "Feel the goods again. Try it on once more, Séamus. You must have this suit for Easter. You'll look so handsome."

"Let me see it on you again, Séamus," my mother says stepping back into the store.

The second try-on always works.

"Eighteen ninety-five," my mother says.

"We'll put cuffs on the pants. No charge."

MY MOTHER ALSO supervises the purchase of my father's clothes. I'm subjected to an expedition into the depths of Manhattan for my suit. When my father needs clothes (rarely) my mother watches for sales at the Fordham Road stores. In the *Bronx Home News* she sees a full-page ad for men's suits at Bonds. An ordinary sale doesn't interest her. She's motivated by "Drastic Year End Reductions" or "Going Out of Business Sale." I go along so she can buy me a new navy blue school sweater. I think she also considers a trip to a sale as another piece of my basic training.

My mother reaches into the racks for something in my father's size. She tells my father he'll look great in this gray-green Glen plaid. "You can add a green silk tie on St Patrick's Day for the Corkmen's dance," she says, carefully noting the price reduction on the sleeve. My father's like me. He just wants to get it over with as quickly as possible. He puts on the jacket. It fits perfectly. My mother points out two pairs of pants on the hanger. My father knows this is the suit she wants him to have. He's good-natured about things like this. He often congratulates her for being tightfisted. At Bonds she can't use her bargaining prowess. The price on the label is not negotiable. She'll be content because she's not paying list price.

My father steps onto a platform to be measured by the tailor. It must be part of Bonds' sales strategy to have a suit fitted in the middle of the store. Potential customers see others buying.

"Your left arm is almost an inch shorter than your right arm," the tailor tells my father.

"That's news to me," my father says bristling.

"It's only a minor adjustment," the tailor says. "You may also need a little tuck, *here*...in the crotch."

"...There's nothing wrong with me *there*," my father hollers. "Keep your friggen suit."

He pulls off his belt, unbuttons the fly and stomps out of the pants. "Bonds' suits are deformed. I'm not." He keeps shaking his finger at the tailor while my mother pushes her underwear-clad husband back into the dressing room.

FOUR

Preparations for Sunday mass start every Saturday afternoon. With wonder I watch my mother orchestrating the proceedings. She gently rolls tufts of my sisters' wet hair into strips of rags and ties off each ratty looking appendage with a knot. How can my sisters sleep with their hair pulled tight by twisted rags?

My sisters and I place our white shoes on the kitchen table where my mother has spread pages of the *New York Daily Mirror*. To fulfill my mother's commandment *no scuffmarks showing* we apply coat after coat of white polish. We line up our shoes. They pass her inspection. My father spit-shines his one pair of black shoes until I can see his face in the toe.

Dinner at five. Now it's ten p.m. We're hungry. My mother makes us hot Ovaltine and sets out two Nabisco chocolate chip cookies for each of us. She tells us again you can't go to communion if you eat one crumb or drink a drop of water after midnight on Saturday.

At seven thirty Sunday morning I hear clocks going off in my sisters' and parents' bedrooms. My sisters and my mother have a lot of female things to do. Since male things are much quicker, my father and I get to doze another half hour.

A mysterious routine in her bedroom transforms my housecoated mother into my father's radiant sweetheart. She selects one of the outfits she has created on her Singer Sewing Machine. It's magical to see a new dress emerge from yards of red and white striped cotton. She arranges the paper pattern on the material, cuts it out with a high degree of efficiency and cost consciousness, brings the miscellaneous pieces of fabric together going up, down and sideways on her foot-peddle sewing machine, cuts buttonholes with a special gizmo, and finishes with meticulous hand stitches. She crowns her costume with one of her sale hats from Alexander's Department Store on Fordham Road. Today she wears a red straw hat with three diminutive white stuffed birds poised for takeoff.

My mother helps my sisters unravel their torturous hairdos. From rag cocoons a dozen quivering ringlets materialize. My mother gently stretches each corkscrew curl and they snap into place.

I dress with my father. I bring my blue seersucker jacket and short pants into his bedroom. He pulls garters up to his knees and snaps in black socks. I put on white short socks. He puts on dark gray serge pants my mother has pressed through a damp dishtowel. I get into my short pants also pressed by my mother to a perfect crease. We each put on a brilliant white shirt stiff as cardboard. On Saturday, my mother bleaches and washes our shirts. She fills a large iron pot with a milky starch concoction, submerges the shirts under the boiling soupy mixture until she knows the paste has permeated the cotton. Then she irons the shirts into an unwrinkled condition taking pains with the collars and my father's French cuffs. My father asks me to slip his only pair of gold-filled Swank cuff links through the double width French cuffs. He pulls one of his two silk ties into the smallest knot he can fashion. I snap a boy's pre-knotted tie into place. My father puts on his matching vest. He takes his father's gold pocket watch from the night table, pries open the back panel to show me the circular photo of my mother, sisters and me taken at Croton-on-the-Hudson a few summers ago. He carefully places the gold watch into his vest pocket saying it's eight forty, time to go. He drapes the chain and fastens the end into a buttonhole. He puts on his gold signet ring with the scripted letter P my mother presented to him on their wedding day. I put on my spotless white shoes and he slips into his black inexpensive Florsheim's with a patent leather glow. My father brushes his wiry hair straight back. I briskly rub a dab of pomade between my palms to liquefy the lotion and smooth it into my hair. I carefully make a part on the left side and comb the hair straight across my brow. We put on our jackets and go into the living room for my mother's examination.

My sisters are near perfection in dresses my mother has sewn. On top of the bouncing curls she has pinned a large pink bow the color of the ribbons she has sewn into their dresses. My mother adjusts my tie and my father's. She spots my cowlick standing straight up and pushes down hard with her palm until it stays in place. She tells us we all look grand.

Pride may be the deadliest sin of all my mother says. But at eight forty five on Sunday morning, walking along Fordham Road to St Nick's with my well turned out mother and father, my two sisters delighting in their finery, and me happy to be a miniature version of my father, I think the O'Flynns are really swell.

FIVE

Our apartment building, 222 Loring Place, is a few feet from the first cross-country highway ever constructed in the United States. Some day, U.S. Highway Number One will take me west over the Harlem River, through Manhattan to the George Washington Bridge, over the Hudson River into New Jersey. A week later I'll be in Los Angeles. I'll love L.A. The sun is always shining, ocean beaches are in the middle of the city, and I may get a glimpse of one of my favorite movie stars; Bela Lugosi, Boris Karloff, Lon Chaney, Jr. If I don't like Los Angeles, I'll return to New York on Highway One, pass along Fordham Road, say hello to my folks, and continue on in an easterly direction through Connecticut, Rhode Island, Massachusetts and end up on the rugged coast of Maine. I have a premonition I'll live someplace near water like my parents did in Southwest Ireland. They could walk to the Atlantic Ocean.

One of my classmates, Danny Brennan, lives in apartment 5C. When we want excitement, we take our families' baby carriages to Safeway. We ask elderly women would you like help with your groceries? We push the carriages to apartment buildings then lug the packages up flights of stairs. They tip at least a nickel, good for a one-way subway fare anywhere in the Bronx, Manhattan, Queens and Brooklyn. In two hours we each net about thirty cents. That's good for a round trip to Manhattan, a Nedick's hotdog and orangeade in Times Square.

There are seven different subways and trains within walking distance of our apartment. East on Fordham Road is the IRT elevated subway. It goes past Yankee Stadium, then underground along Lexington Avenue with stops at the Metropolitan Art Museum and Central Park, then to Times Square. Two blocks further along Fordham is the newer underground IND Line that goes to Rockefeller Center. Three more blocks is the Fordham Road station of the elevated line that travels along Third Avenue in Manhattan. Adjacent to the el on Fordham Road is the New York Central Railroad station. I ride free since my father works for the railroad.

West on Fordham Road is another branch line of the New York Central that runs along the Harlem River, then underground to Grand Central. Or I can walk over the Harlem River Bridge into the northern tip of Manhattan Island where Fordham Road becomes 207th Street, a major stop on two more subway lines. The BMT elevated line goes down the west side of Manhattan to the George Washington Bridge, Museum of Natural History, the Planetarium, Madison Square Garden, Macy's and the Empire State Building. Three blocks west is the IND subway that goes to 125th Street in Harlem, Columbus Circle, and Radio City Music Hall.

Mysteriously, all subways interconnect at various places under Manhattan streets.

WE'RE IN THE lobby of the Empire State Building. We want to go to the top but don't have fifty cents admission. I remember a story in the *New York Daily News* that Olympic athletes from Poland and Czechoslovakia had once tried to develop a new sport running the staircase to the top of the Empire State. We find the stairs near the loading ramp on Thirty Third Street. No one is looking. The door is unlocked. We count 1,576 steps to reach the top. We scratch on the wall:

DANNY BRENNAN & SÉAMUS O'FLYNN

JULY 18, 1941

I see the spires of St Patrick's Cathedral and Central Park. Further north is the end of Manhattan Island where the Hudson and Harlem rivers meet. Fifth Avenue is below and Brooklyn to the east. South is Wall Street and a silhouette of the Statue of Liberty in New York Bay. West the Hudson River and New Jersey. I'm glad I'm not a gawking tourist. This is my city. I live here. My mother and father came to Ellis Island over there. My family's out there now. Uncles, aunts, first cousins. My friends play in those streets. I swim in the Harlem River.

We stay on top for hours. The sun sets over New Jersey. Lights slowly come on unveiling a new shining city.

We ride down on the elevator. No tickets needed.

Each time we climb the stairs we put the date near our first inscription. We start recording the time it takes to run to the top. Best is twenty-eight minutes. We've found New York's best free adventure. All we need is subway fare.

SIX

I'm getting my own bedroom at last. We're moving up one flight from 4C to apartment 5A at 222 Loring, from the dingy back of the building to a bright front apartment that looks across the Harlem River to upper Manhattan and the top of one tower of the George Washington Bridge. The view from our window would really be perfect if I could also see my favorite building, the Empire State.

My own room. It has been my dream for as long as I can remember. A double bed all to myself. Instead of pulling out a couch I just pull back the covers. My bedroom is small but I don't mind. My bed takes up almost all the space in the room. The headboard and the left side of the bed are against walls. A few inches from the right side of the bed is my dresser. There isn't room to open a draw until I climb onto the bed. My closet is three feet wide and only six inches deep. The left side accommodates my dark blue corduroy knickers, one wool sports jacket and my good two-piece suit for Sunday mass. Hanging on the right side are some of my sisters' frilly dresses sewn by my mother.

Fortunately there's no fire escape outside my bedroom window. After a week of feeling very secure, I start thinking a kidnapper could tie a rope to the chimney on the roof and shimmy down a few feet to reach my bedroom. It didn't calm my fears to have my father repeat no one would want me.

Loring Place starts at Fordham Road and climbs up a steep hill. There's an unbroken facade of apartment buildings, four, five and six stories. We're in the first building on the corner. We are the bookend holding up all the other apartment buildings ascending the hill. Now that the war is raging I'm certain when a German rocket knocks out our building, all the buildings up the hill will collapse like a row of dominos, burying 222 Loring for good.

There are definite advantages in the buildings being so close. I have windows to check out before going to bed. I adjust my shade so it's an inch from the windowsill. Just enough room for surveillance. Because of the hill, Ann Corrigan's bedroom window on the fifth floor in the next building is only a few feet higher than mine. The times I do catch her getting ready for bed I can only see from her budding breasts up. Helen Schumacher's bedroom is on the fourth floor directly below Ann Corrigan's. I swear Helen knows I peek at her. Her shade is pulled down about three-quarters of the way. I only see her bottom half. Then there's Dolores Farrell who lives on my floor at 222 who pulls her shade all the way down. Sometimes when a breeze blows her shade back a few inches I can see one breast, one thigh and her patch. A banner night is catching a glimpse of the upper half of Ann, the lower half of Helen and side slices of Dolores.

Then there's the exhibitionist across the alleyway. A fat lady who walks around her apartment without a stitch on, the shades up. Her clothesline stretches from her kitchen window to a neighbor's window. She only hangs one piece of laundry on the line at a time so she can keep coming back throughout the day. Her huge, sagging breasts pile up on the windowsill. She isn't doing it for my benefit. One look is enough. I suspect she's on stage for Mr Hennessey in 3B.

Windows in the neighborhood are wide open on summer nights. In the alleyway sounds echo. I hear the Lexington Avenue el clattering from station to station along Jerome Avenue. Babies cry. Trucks on Fordham Road gear up the steep incline. Toilets flush. A fart. Wailing cats in heat. A sneeze. Laughter. Fans droning. A lonely sob. Springs squeaking. Moans. Pain and pleasure.

MY DRESSER IS the hiding place for three copies of *Esquire* magazine *liberated* from Salerno's Barber Shop on the Grand Concourse. My father uses the word *liberate,* rather than steal. He wouldn't like to think he, or any O'Flynn, would actually steal something. Liberating an item just frees it from its present location. It's just sitting there. If you don't take it someone else will. He doesn't mean taking jewelry from Alexander's Department Store or bag of peanuts from Goldstein's Candy Store. That would be *shoplifting,* a serious crime. My father's second job is as a handyman at the Hastings-on-Hudson Yacht Club. He says a bathing suit left in the steam room at the Yacht Club, then placed in the lost and found box, qualifies as an item that can be *liberated.* Club members have weeks to claim lost articles before they're picked up by the Salvation Army. My father surmises the unclaimed bathing suit would eventually be taken by another club member. Besides they all have plenty of money. We only buy absolute necessities. So bathing suits, sneakers, socks, jocks, T-shirts, sweaters and tennis shorts come home to the O'Flynns via my father's *liberation* policy. If none of us wants these lost odds and ends my mother donates them to the St Vincent de Paul Society.

WE SEE STACKS of *Esquire* magazines and Marvel comics through the window of Salerno's Barber Shop on the Grand Concourse. Mr Salerno is cutting Danny's hair. Since only my father cuts my hair I wait in the shop leafing through comic books. When Mr Salerno's back is to me I *liberate* a few copies of *Esquire* sliding them inside a copy of the *Bronx Home News*. I only take old copies so I can qualify under the guidelines of my father's *liberation* philosophy. Taking a brand new edition of *Esquire* would be stealing, a matter for confession.

The drawings of Varga Girls in *Esquire* are really what we want. Beautiful painted-women, bathing-suit-clad, long-legged. They're contorted, curvy and bursting out of their scanty see-through nightgowns and sparse bathing suits. They're getting into bed. Out of bed. Long legs kicking the air. Showing off heels as high as the Empire State. Or wearing feathered slippers in a Turkish harem. Any moment now they'll explode off the pages of *Esquire* and set fire to my dresser. *"Steam heat,"* says Danny. Certainly no women like them in University Heights or probably nowhere else for that matter. I'm happy to know they are resting comfortably at the bottom of my underwear drawer. If my mother has seen the *Esquires* she never lets on.

MY BRIEF, SAFE, luxurious life is about to end. My mother tells me Cousin Sean Murphy has emigrated from Ireland and will be moving in with us. Just for a while. He has no place to go she explains and he'll pay room and board.

"I guess he'll be using the open-out-couch, right mom," I say.

Silence.

"You don't mean I have to move back into the living room?"

"No, Séamus. But Cousin Sean will share your room for a few weeks."

Sean moved in with me the next day. My mother frees up a few inches on the right side of the closet to make room for Sean's clothes. He thanks me for sharing my room, not knowing I didn't have a choice. The first night he's in my bed I have trouble falling asleep. I've never slept in a bed with anyone before. I hug the wall. In the middle of the night I wake up and hear Sean breathing. I smell sweat and tobacco. I feel strangely peaceful.

Cousin Sean got a job as an elevator operator at Macy's. "I landed in New York three days ago and now work in the world's largest department store," he tells us at dinner. I'm glad because when we are downtown to climb the Empire State Building we also go to Macy's on 34th Street for free food samples at cooking demonstrations.

Cousin Sean thinks New Yorkers are crazy, but very friendly. He also adds to the O'Flynns collection of ghost stories.

"There really is a jack-o'-lantern in the fields around Cork," Sean says. "One night when I was on my way home from a dance I saw a pale yellow light. There was no moon. It was pitch black. I had trouble finding my way. Even though I really didn't want to, I began to follow the elusive light. I noticed it was a lantern and began trailing it through the fields. It floated over rock walls and I followed. I had the feeling I was going in circles for an hour. When I ran faster to see if this was the *will-o'-the-wisp* of legend, the shifting light moved away from me at exactly the same speed. I must have been hypnotized.

I was out of breath and exhausted. I leaned against an oak tree and fell asleep. I got hell from my mother for being out all night. She said my excuse for not coming home was a lot of *malarkey*." Sean is serious. He has terror all over his face when he tells me about fairies and leprechauns. I know he would never lie. I'm glad I live in the Bronx with bright streetlights everywhere and no fire escapes outside my bedroom.

We often hear my father's favorite recollection of his boyhood in Ireland. "I know your story is true, Sean," my father says, "but I have one that may top yours. My mother brought me to Dan Donovan's wake in Benduff. He was a second cousin on my mother's side. He was a hunchback so they had difficulty squeezing him into a small pine box. His sons nailed one of his belts over his ankles and another across his chest, pulling them as tight as possible. He looked grand. As you might expect in Cork there was much eating and drinking. I was fourteen and bored. I found a straight razor and surreptitiously began cutting the belt that was over Donovan's chest. Finally the last strand of leather gave way. Donovan slowly sat up in the casket. The Lord preserve us screamed Mrs Donovan. Sure it's Lazarus himself, said Father Collins. The cottage emptied out in seconds."

My mother had her own experience with ghosts. "I was walking to school with my sister Margaret when we heard horses and a carriage coming up behind us. Without turning around I knew a horse-drawn hearse was on the way to Calvary cemetery down the road. But when I looked back there was nothing to be seen. It was a bright, sunny day. We could hear horses coming closer and closer. There wasn't any dust, just hoof beats and a rattling carriage. I tried to take Margaret's hand but couldn't. We were being separated against our will. We were forced to opposite sides of the road. We started to cry. I told her to get off the road as quickly as possible. The hearse passed between us. Only then could we get back to the center of the road. We hugged each other. No one to this day believes this actually happened. But it did."

Tonight I'm glad a boarder is sharing my bed.

SEVEN

YOU NO GOOD FUCKING BASTARD. OOHHHHH. I'LL GET MY GUN AND KILL YOU. YOU BITCH.

The Sweeneys in 5B are drunk again.

The O'Flynn apartment has a fifty-foot common wall with the Sweeneys. Both apartments are identical, with a reverse plan.

Mr Sweeney is a retired policeman. After her seven children left home, Mrs Sweeney started drinking heavily. I pass her coming up the stairs. The paper bag she clutches is twisted in the shape of a bottle. *"Helloooo Shaaymusss"* she says in a thick brogue. She leaves a faint odor of vomit hanging in the air. "Lovely day now isn't it, *Shaaymusss.*"

I know we're in for another night of terror.

My father worries about Mr Sweeney's revolver. Retired policemen don't have to turn in their guns. My father says one day he'll make good on the threats he blusters to his wife.

The Sweeneys have separate bedrooms. Mrs Sweeney is in the larger bedroom on the street side. It's exactly like my parents. Mr Sweeney has the reverse duplicate of my bedroom, with only a few inches of plaster wall between us. I can hear him snoring through the wall after they shriek at each other for hours down the long hallway.

"YOU NO GOOD IRISH SOT."

"SHUT YOUR MOUTH OR I'LL SEND YOU TO THE UNDERTAKER."

I put my head under the pillow. My father tells me Mr Sweeney was an excellent shot when he served with New York's Finest. He was decorated many times. My father reasons if his gun goes off the bullet will find Mrs Sweeney. And if he misses her, the bullet will probably not come through the thick plaster into our apartment. What concerns me is my father says *probably not.* In the movies a bullet takes out everything in its way. I know a bullet will easily rip through the plaster hallway but I don't think it will have enough juice to then tear a hole in my bedroom wall. I begin to believe I'm reasonably safe.

The Sweeneys aren't always drunk. I see them at mass and hope Holy Communion will help them forget their demons. God performs miracles all the time. And they do have good days. When their children and grandchildren visit, laughter comes through the wall.

IN AUGUST 1941 my parents say there'll be a new baby O'Flynn in a few weeks. I didn't notice my mother growing under her loose housedresses.

Now I'll have to move back to the living room and the pull-out-bed.

"Don't be concerned, Séamus," my mother says. "We're going to follow my parents' example and put a crib next to our bed so our new baby will be close."

"I'm glad we're having a baby," my sister Siobhan says. "I've wondered why we have the smallest family in our building."

"Since Sinead was born in 1933, I've had three miscarriages," my mother says. "A miscarriage means the baby is tiny, the size of say a one cent Tootsie Roll. It doesn't stay inside because something's wrong."

The baby is born at Flower Fifth Avenue Hospital in Manhattan. Two weeks have passed. My mother and baby sister are still in the hospital.

My father tells us my mother isn't feeling well but the baby's doing just fine. A week later my mother arrives in a taxi at the entrance to 222 Loring. My father puts a wooden kitchen chair on the sidewalk. Sinead carries her new baby sister upstairs. My mother sits on the chair and my father and Mr Hanrahan from IB carry her up the five flights. She goes to bed immediately.

I learn my mother had been hemorrhaging. It stopped for a while. One night when the hemorrhaging began again my mother kept ringing her buzzer but the nurse didn't respond. Finally a woman in the next bed crawled down the hallway for help.

"Did she almost die?" my sister Siobhan asks.

"Yes, it was a nightmare for a few days," my father says. "But she's recovering now." My mother is too weak to go to the christening, but she chooses the name Marita in honor of the Virgin Mary and St Rita. My mother has a devotion to St Rita, a mystical Augustinian nun who lived in the fifteenth century. When we complain we're hurt, she says you have no idea of real pain compared to St Rita's suffering. After her husband was murdered and two sons died of fever, Rita wanted to enter the Augustinian convent in Cascia, Italy. The Mother Superior turned her down because she wasn't a virgin. After praying for months, one night she saw three figures in the shadows outside her house. They beckoned her to follow. She realized they were St John the Baptist, St Augustine and St Nicholas of Tolentine. They miraculously passed through the convent walls and clothed her in the habit of the Augustinian nuns. When the Mother Superior discovered Rita inside the convent walls, she let her stay. A few years later while praying before a large crucifix, asking to share a small part of Christ's suffering, a piece of thorn fell from the crown on the crucifix and entered deep into her forehead where it stayed the rest of her life. My mother says after St Rita died in the early sixteen hundreds, many miracles were performed through her intercession. The Church named her the Saint of Desperate Causes. "It's good St Rita's around," my mother says, "in case an incurable illness comes our way."

When Father Kruger hears the new O'Flynn baby's name, he says she can't be called Marita. There's no Saint Marita.

Father Kruger scolds my father. "Your other three children don't have saints' names, Sinead, Séamus, Siobhan. They are Irish, but not saints. You got away with it because there was a lax priest at your former parish, St Luke. I know him and he is still cutting corners."

My father tries to convince the pastor saying my mother would be cheered up to have the baby named Marita. My father says right here in St Nick's there's a statue of St Rita over there near the one of the Virgin Mary. She's an Augustinian like you are Father. Kruger says again there's no Saint Marita, so the baby will be called Mary and Rita. Father Kruger says Mary Rita is the name period, or she won't be christened. I think my father is ready to call off the baptism but he knows my mother will be more upset if the baby isn't christened at all. If Mary Rita dies before baptism she'll go to limbo for eternity and never see the face of God. Sounds like a cruel God to me. This new baby, a few days old is stained with original sin, the first sin ever committed when Eve coaxed Adam to eat the forbidden fruit.

When my father places the new Catholic baby in my mother's arms she says she likes Mary Rita as much as Marita. Besides, Marita does sound a *wee bit Italian.*

ABOUT A YEAR later I find a red covered book on my parents' dresser, RHYTHM. I know what rhythm is all about. If you have it, you jitterbug well and sing like Frank Sinatra. When I see the word IMPRIMATUR I know it isn't about music at all. It's a church approved official Catholic document.

RHYTHM is strange. There are only a few days when it's safe to do it. There are eggs and sperm and the idea is to trick them into not being around at the same time. A thermometer is necessary. When baby Mary Rita has a fever, my mother puts the thermometer in her bottom. When she puts the same thermometer under her own tongue it tells my mother if her eggs are fresh. It seems RHYTHM tells my mother she's ready. I suppose a man like my father is always ready. If both are ready RHYTHM says you can't do anything right now. Too confusing. RHYTHM must have confused my mother and father too. Shortly after, my mother was pregnant again.

UNCLE GREGORY, MY mother's youngest brother, came for his favorite Sunday dinner of leg of lamb with my mother's home made mint and vinegar sauce on December 7, 1941.

"I can't believe it. I can't believe they could sneak up on us like this," he says.

We're listening to the radio. "At 7:48 a.m. this morning the Japanese Navy and Air Force attacked Pearl Harbor destroying one hundred seventy planes, eight battleships, three light cruisers, and three destroyers. There was a heavy loss of American life..."

"President Roosevelt will declare war tomorrow," Uncle Gregory says. "They take the youngest men first, but I won't wait till they reach my age, thirty. I'm going to join up right away."

"Now don't make such a hasty decision," my mother says.

"I love this country. It would be an honor to help America. Half of George Washington's army during the Revolution was Irish," Uncle Gregory says. "Irishmen have fought in all of America's wars. I wish I'd been around in 1776. I would have enjoyed kicking the English out of America, forever."

Three days after Pearl Harbor, the country had its first war hero. A twenty-six year old Westpointer, Captain Colin Kelly Jr. flew his B-17 to attack a Japanese Naval Task Force near the Philippines. The Flying Fortress had a direct hit on the battleship Haruna sending it to the bottom. Two Japanese Zeros attacked Kelly's plane from the rear. Fire flashed through the plane. Captain Kelly ordered his crew to bail out. Before he could follow, the B-17 exploded. My Uncle Gregory says Kelly's heroism is a sign to him. "In a war that's just beginning," he says, "America has its first hero, an Irish Catholic. I'm following him into the armed forces."

THE MENDELSSON FAMILY has moved into apartment 1C. My father says they're running away from Hitler. My mother says when they came from Germany they should have moved to one of the Jewish neighborhoods along the Grand Concourse. The Mendelssons must have been surprised when they put their name on their mailbox. They saw nineteen other mailboxes with Irish names. Once you sign a year's lease you can't move.

While Irish reels have played on Victrolas at 222 Loring, the melodies of Esther Mendelsson's classical piano now reverberate through the halls. The O'Flynns eat plain food, meat and potatoes, and mandatory fish on Friday. From 1C there are strange aromas, like vinegar or something pickled seeping into the hallway.

Everett Mendelsson is my age. He goes to P.S. 92 a few blocks away. He goes to the synagogue on Saturday; I go to St Nick's on Sunday. He takes violin lessons, I play stickball and baseball. We have nothing in common. Except we're both boys and as it turns out that's enough.

We become friends. The Mendelsson's apartment is crammed with beautiful objects, some antiques from the old country, oriental rugs, overflowing bookcases in every room. Mr Mendelsson, who had been a curator of a Berlin museum, opened a stamp collecting shop on Fordham Road.

Everett tells me his sister Esther isn't feeling good and asks if I'd like to use her ticket to go to the American Museum of Natural History. We walk over the bridge into Manhattan and take the BMT downtown. There's a film and lecture by a couple that had lived along the Amazon. We visit the dinosaur exhibit; see stuffed birds, reptiles and insects. It's more exciting than sitting in a classroom.

New York museums are free. The Mendelssons have subscriptions to lecture series. When someone in the family can't go, I accompany them to the Hayden Planetarium, Museum of Natural History and most often to the Metropolitan Museum of Art. When I say my nightly prayers I'm tempted to pray one of the Mendelssons will get sick this week.

The Mendelssons have a car. They're going to spend a weekend at a friend's farm in Putnam County. I'm invited. After driving a few miles out of the Bronx, the parkway winds through heavily forested areas. I'm surprised to see the number of apartment buildings decrease. Now I see private homes through the trees. The Bronx fades away. The Taconic Parkway takes us to Mahopac Falls. The Silverstein's farmhouse is not in good repair, but no one seems to mind. We sleep wrapped in comforters in the barn. The only cows I've ever seen were at the Borden's Dairy World of Tomorrow at the 1939 World's Fair. Everett has experienced country life outside Berlin. He's delighted at my reaction to a cow giving milk and taking a steaming dump at the same time. The countryside, the sounds, aromas, animals, carrots pulled from the ground for dinner, home grown lettuce and radishes. Everything that weekend is startlingly different.

Mrs Mendelsson asks me if I have an inkling of what kind of work I'll do when I grow up. Her children have already picked careers. Esther wants to be a teacher. Everett hopes to get accepted by the Bronx High School of Science. The only decision I've made is what I don't want to be, a cop, fireman or railroad worker like my father. I tell my Uncle Gregory I enjoy writing stories like he does. He doesn't think writers make enough to live on, unless you write clever advertisements for the *Saturday Evening Post* or *Life Magazine*.

When their lease is up, the Mendelssons move to the Mosholu Parkway section of the Bronx. I wonder what they think of the year they lived within the boundaries of St Nick's parish? Why are so many cracks made about Jews? The only Jewish family I've ever known opened my world and changed my life. I never saw Everett again.

EIGHT

We have new supers," my father says at dinner. "Michael and Sheila McCarthy from County Kerry. I think he's an alcoholic."

"How can you tell?" my mother asks.

"His wife is strong and healthy and pretty," he says. "But Mike is frail, downright skinny, shaky, eyes glassy. He didn't look up when I said hello. Definitely a drinking problem."

"Because you're skinny doesn't mean you're a drunk," I say.

"Séamus, it's none of your business," my father says.

"Who else would take a job as superintendent," my mother says. "It's worse than working in a quarry."

"Mr McCarthy continues the 222 Loring superintendent's tradition of a long line of lushes from the old sod," my father says.

The landlord of 222, who has an office on the Grand Concourse, gives the super a rent-free basement apartment and some cash. They're supposed to sweep five floors of hallways and steps every day, wet mop a few times a week, and shovel coal into the furnace providing steam heat and hot water. Every night at six the super rings the dumbwaiter bell to collect garbage.

"My dad says Mr McCarthy is a sot," I tell Danny. "Let's peek in his window."

We climb over the fence into the back of the building and hide in the scraggly bushes.

"There he is," says Danny. "Your dad's right. He has a bottle of beer in his hand and he's wobbly."

McCarthy peers at us. "I think he sees our flashlight. Let's get out of here."

We scoot in a side door and hide in the trunk room behind a row of baby carriages. The light goes on.

"Who's in there? You bastards. Spying on me. Where are you?"

"He can't grab us," Danny whispers. "He's woozy. Let's dart by him."

Danny skips by, but McCarthy grabs my arm. He drops his beer bottle and has me in a bear hug.

"We're just playing a game. Hiding in the trunk room. We always do it."

"You live here?" McCarthy slurs through a mouthful of stinking brown teeth.

"Yes. O'Flynn. Fifth floor."

"Well fifth floor O'Flynn, I'm going to show you what will happen if I catch you nosing on us again."

He pulls me through a maze of sooty-whitewashed cement walls lighted with low watt bare bulbs.

"This is where you'll end up, you little prick." He clanks open the iron door of the huge furnace. He pops his cigarette into the red-hot hole. It disintegrates before hitting the burning coals. I've never seen inside a furnace. Endless live coals flashing tongues of blue and orange flames.

"I'll fricassee your ass. There'll be nothing left. No corpse to get rid of. Ha. Ha. Dimwit O'Flynn will end up in one of our ash cans at the curb."

I feel sick. His stench comes from his decaying liver. Rotting liver, rotting gums.

I yank free. When I reach the fifth floor I'm burning up and still my teeth are clattering like it was a below freezing winter day.

IT'S THREE A.M. when the gun goes off. I move my hand along my headboard searching for a hole.

"He's shot Mrs Sweeney," my father shouts running down the hall to my room.

"Are you O.K., Séamus?"

"I think so. Is she dead?"

"I'm going to call the police."

"But dad, he *is* the police."

My father puts his ear against the hallway wall. He can hear Mrs Sweeney moaning, crying. "She must be in her death throws. That bastard. How could he shoot the mother of his children? May God have mercy on her."

"Maybe she's just wounded. I only heard one shot."

Phones ring. Everyone in the building is awake. But no one opens their hall doors. My mother says Mr Sweeney could run amuck. She checks the double locks on the front door.

"My God," she says. "We share the same fire escape. He could climb out his bedroom window and break into our bedroom. Paddy, check the lock on our window." My mother starts sobbing, moves us into the kitchen, away from the hallway and Mr Sweeney.

"He's finally done it," my mother yells across the alleyway to Mrs Donovan, who's peering out her kitchen window.

"Lord help us," Mrs Donovan cries, pulling back from the window. "We could be next. He can come down the fire escape."

The police car jumps the curb and stops at the apartment entrance.

"Apartment 5B," my father screeches from our living room window. "Hurry."

They bang on the Sweeney's door. No response.

We can hear Mrs Sweeney's sobs. They're louder now.

"She must still be alive," my mother says.

They carry the body down the five flights. My father doesn't believe the police when they tell him it's Mr Sweeney who is dead. The gun is clenched in his fist. The bullet went through his head and into his bedroom ceiling.

I don't remember another time like this when every apartment door at 222 is open. Neighbors pack the landings and stairs. I guess no one really liked the Sweeneys. Maybe they were an embarrassment, being Irish. Now there will be less noise in the alley on summer nights.

NINE

I met my grandparents only once. I was one when my mother took my sister Siobhan and me to Ireland on an ocean liner to visit her mother and my paternal grandparents. My mother told me how they loved squeezing the baby Yank's plump arms and legs.

My mother never saw her mother again.

My grandparents were three thousand miles away in Southwest Cork. I have a sepia-toned photo of my maternal grandmother Marguerite O'Leary holding me on a donkey with a large whitewashed house in the background. My mother's grandfather Peter Hayes was born in that house in 1827. My grandmother was born there in 1870 and my mother in 1904. We have no photos of the O'Flynn grandparents. But they have a photo of my sisters and me hanging in their cottage near the Benduff slate quarry.

When I told my mother I wished I had a grandmother in New York, she said her own heart was much heavier than mine.

"I'll never be able to afford another trip home," my mother said.

Her parents built a crib beside their bed to keep each new baby nearby. A month after they had their ninth child, Grandfather O'Leary died at forty-one. A horse had kicked him in the stomach. The wound turned to cancer. Alone, my grandmother had to raise her brood and run the fifty-acre family dairy farm.

When she was eighteen the only work my mother could find was as a live-in housekeeper in Cork City. She decided to go to America in 1923 with her brothers Harry twenty-two and Sonny, twenty. She took a course in typing so she wouldn't have to take a position as a housekeeper when she went to the states.

"On our last night home we had an *American wake*," my mother said. "The party was a sad affair. My brothers and I were *the dead* being mourned. We're going to the states. My mother knew she would probably never see her three children again. I'll never forget the last hours with her as she prayed a blessing on her emigrating children."

They sailed from Queenstown in Cobh Harbor in the southern part of County Cork. A New York cousin Ella O'Brien, working as a maid on Park Avenue, let them sleep on the floor of her cold water flat at 219 West 25th Street, in Hell's Kitchen. Ella warned them as they set out to find work there are still some New York businesses posting NO IRISH NEED APPLY signs.

By noon the next day all three had found work. Their Irish dreams were already coming true. Harry was employed in the baggage room of Pennsylvania Station and Sonny a shipping clerk at Macy's Department Store on Thirty-Fourth Street. Since my mother could type she was hired by a printing concern on South Broadway. They could walk to their new jobs.

Harry, on his fifth day of work, looked up through a partially opened door. An elevator coming down hit him on the head and knocked him to the bottom of the shaft. My mother and Sonny were in New York less than a week and they were in the City Mortuary claiming Harry. The death certificate showed the cause of death was "crushing of head, struck accidentally by an elevator on August 5, 1923 at 1:20 p.m." My mother's eyes still mist when she recalls those first days as immigrants. My mother couldn't believe there wasn't a Catholic cemetery in downtown Manhattan. Everywhere in Ireland there's a cemetery within walking distance. They borrowed from relatives to buy a plot in Calvary Cemetery in Queens. My mother wondered why Harry had to be buried so far from West 25th Street.

"I quit the job I had just taken. I spent the next two weeks walking the unfamiliar streets of New York City keening for Harry," my mother recalls.

Finally she wrote to her mother. She had just said farewell to three of her children a few weeks ago and now she had lost a son.

MY FATHER GOT his dander up when he told us about his immigration. For as long as anyone could remember the O'Flynns worked in the Benduff Slate Quarries in Skibbereen, County Cork. Owned by English gentry, the quarry had been in operation since 1830. When my father's grandfather Michael O'Flynn was forty-nine he was killed in a quarry cave-in in 1892 along with seven others aged thirteen to sixty-two. My father, usually a gentle man, got fighting mad when he described the dangerous conditions at the quarry. His father John O'Flynn narrowly missed being killed when another ledge gave way in 1919. My grandmother Julia O'Flynn noticing the beginnings of miner's lung disease in her husband and fearful another mishap at the quarry could claim her five sons, planted the notion of emigration at an early age.

"For ninety years the O'Flynns worked in the quarry," my father said. "They knew it was dangerous work. When they noticed a cleavage developing and reported the potential disaster to the owners, they were given the option of work, or the gate. The fear of hunger always overcame their fear of danger."

My father emigrated at twenty in 1924 with his two brothers Jim, twenty-two, and Mike, twenty-three. The two brothers remaining in Ireland continued to work in the quarry. The three O'Flynns traveled steerage to Ellis Island.

My father never saw his parents again.

MY MOTHER WEPT quietly. She was reading a letter from her sisters in Ireland. Her mother died last Sunday. My mother took a pressed white rose from the envelope. She deeply breathed in the remaining fragrance and then placed it under my nose.

The O'Flynns had cousins who arrived in America in the mid-eighteen hundreds just after the devastating Potato Famine had taken the lives of almost one million Irishmen. Many railroad lines at the time were under construction throughout the eastern United States. Immigrants were eagerly sought to work for the rapidly expanding railroads.

While planning his emigration, my father thought he would first try to find work with an American railroad. The New York Central Railroad hired him as a third-rail man. His gang inspects and repairs thirty miles of track running along the Harlem River, up the Hudson River to the Croton Roundhouse. He begins each day walking downhill four blocks to the Fordham Road station of the New York Central.

My father completed elementary school in Ireland, but did not go to high school. He enjoys his railroad job. He likes working outdoors repairing faulty sections of the third rail, which carries electric current to run the trains. My father's only grumble is he hasn't been promoted to foreman. A dozen men are in his gang. Over a twenty year period you think someone would notice him. But he says railroad work is better than getting lung disease in the quarry. And the whole O'Flynn family can ride free from Manhattan to Chicago, even though we've never been north of Albany. My father says it's fine to have free passes but once we arrive in Chicago he couldn't afford a hotel.

When my father knows he'll be working on tracks below Riverdale, he brings a fishing pole folded inside his lunch box. Englewood Cliffs and the Palisades are directly opposite on the New Jersey side of the Hudson. My father finds worms easily, scratching under the railroad ties. He casts into the river and then wedges the rod into the rocks. He opens his lunch box and eats the sandwich my mother has made. He sips tea from his Thermos top. My mother whispers her hope my father doesn't bring another fish home. It will be a Hudson River eel or a polluted striped bass. There are *strange things* moving on the surface of the river. She's certain the murky water has soaked right through the skin. God only knows what the fish might have swallowed.

My father loves to explain the life cycle of Hudson eels. They live most of their lives in fresh water in the northern reaches of the Hudson River three hundred miles from New

York City. After ten years or so, a miraculous transition takes place every autumn. Some eels turn from yellow-green to beautiful metallic silver. This is their signal to head back to their birthplace. They make the pilgrimage down the Hudson to New York Bay into the salty Atlantic Ocean. They journey to the warm Sargasso Sea, south of Bermuda, to spawn. Then both female and male die.

It is autumn again. We're tight-lipped when my father unrolls the stinking newspaper on the kitchen table. We hope his catch is striped bass because the way my mother prepares it, is easy to get down. *Oh, no.* Two silver eels, still kicking. My sisters and I think they are the world's ugliest creatures. My father grabs a wiggling eel. It slips from his grip and lands on the linoleum. Sinead screams. "It's a snake. It's coming at me."

My father cuts a circle around the eel's neck and snaps the skin off. Then he cuts off the head. Soon there are small circles of cracker-crumbed-snake-like-fried-eel on our dinner plates. My sisters and I won't finish dinner tonight. My mother tells us once more about the starving children in Europe who would love to have the leftovers from our bountiful table. She tells us it tastes just like tender chicken. Since we can't leave until our plates are clean we save the most unappetizing morsels for the end. When my father isn't looking, we stuff the repugnant fishy pieces inside our cheeks, get permission to leave the table and dash to the bathroom. My father doesn't know it, but my sisters and I have hardly tasted Hudson-Harlem River eel.

My father has a deep tan on the upper half of his body. My mother says you can tell a laboring man by his tanned chest and back and milk white legs. She points out other working men at Orchard Beach and Rockaway. She insists my father get a sun tan on his bottom half too. On summer days, after lunch, he strips and stretches out naked on the rocks hoping the passing New York Central passengers do not see him. To cool off he carefully lowers himself into the river. Like most Irishmen he can't swim. He holds onto a rock and kicks his legs.

My father is proud of his dark red wavy hair. A few days before he goes to the barber he heats olive oil in a saucer. My sister Siobhan gives his hair an oil massage. She combs a few hairs to the side and gently dips a cotton ball into the hot olive oil and dabs his scalp. When his head is dripping oil, my sister runs a black Ace fine toothcomb through his hair.

"Rub my scalp as hard as you can," he tells my sister.

My mother says my father fears he will be bald at an early age. So far he hasn't lost any hair so he's certain hot olive oil treatments are lubricating the roots.

At night I see my father on his knees praying at the side of his bed. When he finishes breakfast he kneels on a wooden kitchen chair, closes his eyes, lowers his head and silently prays for a few moments. He makes the sign of the cross, kisses my mother and grabs his lunch pail.

A lifetime of lifting rails and railroad ties keeps my father trim. He has a long straight nose with a slight rise at the tip and a large mouth. Melancholy green eyes. His deep red hair is beginning to streak with gray.

Like most immigrants, my father has two jobs. Coming home from working along the railroad tracks, he washes off the day's grime, changes into clean work clothes, has dinner, and heads down the hill to catch the 6:20 New York Central commuter train to Westchester. At night and on weekends he's a handyman at the Hastings-on-Hudson Yacht Club.

At the north end of the Hastings-on-Hudson station a bridge crosses the tracks leading to the Yacht Club gate. It isn't really a yacht club. The dock jutting into the Hudson has only six small boats tied-up. It's actually a tennis club. My father rolls the clay tennis courts, cleans the pool and keeps the squash court in good order.

After school I help my father roll the clay courts. When the club closes at night my father lets me swim in the outdoor heated pool. On weekends I pull up weeds at the club. My father tells me Mr Hargrave who just got out of the pool is a bigwig at the First National City Bank of Manhattan. He lives next door to Arturo Toscanini the famous conductor. I walk up the winding lanes of Hastings-on-Hudson above the club, peering through gates at mansions overlooking the Hudson River.

THERE'S A PHOTO in my parent's bedroom taken on their wedding day in 1927. My father looks happy. My mother's not smiling. Is she peaceful, or is she worried? She may be thinking of her new life in America, so far from home. She could be mother to six, eight, ten. Her own mother had nine, one each year until her husband died.

In Ireland my mother and father lived only a few miles apart. Although my mother says they never met, my father swears he remembers seeing my mother at a dance in the parish hall. He says he remembers her long brown wavy hair.

"I'm disappointed you're marrying Patrick O'Flynn," her mother wrote. She reminds my mother the O'Flynn family still lives in a one-room cottage with an outhouse in the quarry town of Benduff. She says anyone without a farm in Ireland is poor. As a final discouragement she mentions my grandmother and Patrick's father are actually cousins. "You'll be marrying your second cousin. Won't the church have something to say about that?"

My mother says her mother forgot to mention Patrick is a devout church-going Irishman with a steady paycheck from the prestigious New York Central Railroad. She should be glad she's not marrying an American Protestant. For their weekend honeymoon, Patrick and Kathleen ride a New York Central train along the Water Level Route to Niagara Falls.

MY MOTHER HAS deep-set determined gray eyes. She parts her hair in the middle and pins it back in a bun. She may be out of breath doing laundry but she always greets you with her serene smile. Every day my mother bends over the bathroom tub pulling and pushing my father's filthy work clothes across a corrugated metal scrubbing board. She proudly shows us the muscle in her right arm saying it's almost as big as my father's. Almost as hard as his too. She's thankful the landlord supplies hot water. She says we couldn't afford all the hot water we use. She takes a sheet and wrings it out with her strong hands until it's too tight to unravel. When the first laundry basket is full she carries it to the roof. She shakes out each crushed piece of laundry and hangs it on clotheslines stretching across the tar roof of the apartment building. She only complains in winter when the laundry freezes on the line. I help her carry frozen sheets and clothes back to the apartment. My father's denim work clothes are the hardest to soften up. I lean his frozen pants against the radiator. Then I put his stiff work shirt on top. I create his head out of newspapers and crown it with one of his caps. An old pair of work shoes completes the mock-up. Steam heat starts the thawing. The head sinks into the shirt and tumbles into the pants.

My father uses the winter laundry to pull a *shenanigan* on my mother. He takes her frozen girdle, sets it on a straight chair and covers it with one of her ice-cold slips. On her paper head he props one of her outrageous feathered hats.

My mother scrubs my father every day. When he comes home at five-thirty he's grimy from outdoor work. He goes into the bathroom, starts running the water in the tub, takes his clothes off and calls my mother. She soaps a washcloth and moves it back and forth across his back. She cradles his arm as if it was a baby's and carefully washes each finger.

My father isn't shy. Perhaps he wants his family to see the grubby reminders of his workday. When his back is clean he stands up. My mother gently moves the washcloth over his backside and his *shillelagh* (his name for it) and then briskly scrubs his strong white legs. He sits down in the gray soapy water. My mother massages shampoo into his hair. She closes the curtain so he can lie back in the hot water and then take a shower.

I don't remember my mother ever being sick. She's certain her good health is the result of years of climbing five flights of stairs, two or three times a day. When she's tired she puts the groceries on the dumbwaiter in the basement. Once in the apartment she pulls the dumbwaiter up to the fifth floor and takes her packages off. When we come home from school she is often napping.

MY MOTHER IS a splendid seamstress. She keeps her 1926 model foot-pedal Singer sewing machine with a vibrating shuttle between her bed and the large window facing west. She makes everything for my sisters and herself, except stockings and underwear. If McCall's doesn't make a paper pattern for an article of clothing my mother asks my father to create one out of brown wrapping paper. She orders everything else she needs from the Sears Roebuck catalog. She told me once everything I had on was from Sears, including my sneakers.

My mother's seamstress skills are in demand. A nurses' uniform store near the Grand Concourse hired her to do alterations. Now nurses come to apartment 5A for fittings. One of the nurses introduced my mother to the Corkmen's Association of New York. They need fifty new costumes for next year's St Patrick's Day parade. Why not hire a seamstress who comes from Cork? Soon bolts of white, green and gold satin are stored under all the beds in our apartment. The costume worn by mothers and daughters in the parade includes a green dress and a cape with one white satin side and the other gold. My mother patiently sews intricate gold sequin designs on each cape. A seaman's style cap of green and gold completes the outfit. From September until the day before St Patrick's Day she cuts and sews Corkmen's costumes. In a few years she has outfitted two hundred women. After we march on St Patrick's Day with St Nicholas School, our family sits on the Fifth Avenue grandstand and applauds wildly when the colorful Corkmen's Association marches by. The mothers and daughters look grand my father says. We have a lot of extra dollars on March 18th.

TEN

The axis of the Fordham Road-University neighborhood is St Nicholas of Tolentine Church. Everyone and everything whirls around the cathedral-like limestone Gothic church proudly rooted at the intersection of U.S. Highway One, Fordham Road and University Avenue. The church's twelve story high twin towers dominate five and six story apartment buildings in every direction. At night St Nicholas' great rose window glows like a massive eye overseeing twenty thousand parishioners.

When Fordham Road was an unpaved country thoroughfare in 1905, the Archdiocese of New York purchased the church property. Immigrants were still pouring into New York. The city's subways and elevated trains brought the new arrivals further north out of the lower East Side and Hell's Kitchen to the northern boundaries of the city where rents were much less expensive.

The new parish of St Nicholas extended from the Harlem River in the west to the Jerome Park Reservoir-Chaflìln Estate on the north. Two blocks south of the new parish was New York University's Bronx campus, already a landmark at the turn of the century in the wide-open countryside. At the time there was only one apartment house in the neighborhood, 2405 Grand Avenue and a few private homes.

The four lots purchased by Archbishop Farley originally belonged to local Indians who called the area *Kekeshick*. They sold the property to the Dutch West India Company and eventually to the Protestant Dutch Church of the City of New York. It had been in the hands of the Lewis Morris family from 1775 to 1905.

After World War I there was a period of national prosperity. Hundreds of apartment buildings were constructed in the University Heights section of the Bronx. It was *the* new place for immigrants to live.

At the Kingsbridge Public Library I glanced through art books on the great cathedrals of Europe. Cathedrals are the most impressive and tallest buildings in their cities and towns. Most of the families in St Nick's parish are immigrants. In the old country, the church was the center of their lives. St Nicholas parish has more people living within its boundaries than many cathedral towns in England, France and Italy.

EVERY SUNDAY AT St Nick's is like a subway rush hour. A crush of people coming out and going in church doors. Crowds push and shove to get into the main church building. Once the pews are full, the doors are locked, and latecomers rush downstairs to the basement church. At the last two masses, eleven a.m. and twelve noon, both churches fill up quickly and the overflow walk down the street, past the convent, to hear mass in the school auditorium.

Since most fathers have two jobs, there's always sufficient income to pay rent, feed the family and still drop a weekly contribution into the collection basket. My father gives my sisters and me a penny or two to include in the collection. Sheer numbers keep the parish treasury overflowing. Income is supplemented with weekly bingo games, raffle books, a yearly weeklong bazaar, holy day collections, novenas, weddings, funerals. The basket is passed at every opportunity. My father was in the rectory one Sunday evening and swears he heard coin-sorting machines running in the basement. Rumors persist the Augustinian priests send some of the excess parish funds to the Pope and Augustinian missions around the world.

The school has twenty-four classrooms, three for each grade at the elementary level. The parish's high school follows Catholic wisdom, keeping boys and girls apart in their teens. They can flirt as they pass in the hallways but they are never in the same classroom. The Dominican Sisters staff the elementary school and also teach girls in high school. The DeLaSalle Christian Brothers instruct boys in high school, plus a few Augustinian priests. There's no tuition. Costs are covered through the Sunday collection. The priests and nuns are committed to educate children of immigrants and instruct them in the faith.

Everyone I know is Catholic. Now that the Mendelssons have moved, everyone at 222 is Catholic. All relatives in Ireland are Catholic. The O'Flynn line of *mackerel-snappers* is traced to 1865 when my great-great grandfather Henry O'Leary, who was Church of England, converted to Roman Catholic when he married Nora Daly.

Christian symbols are everywhere. All parish buildings are oversized; the enormous church, elementary school, high school, rectory, convent, gymnasium. At noon the Angelus bell chiming *Ave Maria* from the church tower can be heard a mile in every direction. I'm in the parish school all day, in church every Sunday and my parents even take my sisters and me to hour-long weeknight novenas. I wake up with a prayer and I'm on my knees before hopping into bed. School begins with the Pledge of Allegiance to the flag of the United States, then a daily prayer led by a nun who gives us an hour of religious instruction in the Catholic Baltimore Catechism. Priests occasionally squeeze in a weekday mass for special anniversaries like the feast days of St Augustine or St Dominic. The nine a.m. Sunday mass is crammed with all the children from the elementary and high schools. At home we say *Grace Before Meals*. My parents sometimes gather us in the living room and lead us in the rosary, which takes fifteen minutes from playtime. I pray enough. I don't need extra prayers in the middle of the day.

Crucifixes are on top of the church, in the corridors of the school, on our uniforms, around nuns' necks, on the classroom wall, above my bed.

A free Catholic calendar is distributed to every family by Rafferty Brothers Funeral Parlor across from the church on University Avenue. It hangs above the kitchen table sending out daily messages in bright red ink, like Holy Days (mandatory mass even on a week day), and marks the birthdays of saints. The first Holy Day is January 1, Feast of the Circumcision, which I think is a strange reason to have to go to church. I'm circumcised, but to have celebrated for twenty centuries the cutting off of Jesus' foreskin makes me smile. It helps take him out of the realm of the ethereal and gives him a *shillelagh* like me. I like that.

IN THE SIXTH grade, Sister Rose of the Precious Blood selects me to be an altar boy candidate. This will cut into my stickball and baseball time and my Saturday delivery business at Safeway. My parents insist. So I begin the study of the mass in Latin. I have to learn the complete Our Father in Latin, and *The Suscipiat*, a long complex prayer that makes no sense to me. Fortunately many responses I have to learn are just *Amen*. When I say *The Mea Culpa* I pound my heart three times with my fist closed. Sister Rose also tells me if I do a good job I can serve as an altar boy at weddings. Other altar boys have told me after a wedding mass everyone is in a jubilant mood. You hang around and keep smiling at the best man, waiting for him to remember your tip. It's at least a dollar for an hour's work. That's what I make in a month of Saturdays delivering groceries at Safeway. Funerals are a bummer. Everyone is crying and sad. No tips for altar boys.

After weeks of memorization I pass the Latin exam. I'm assigned a locker in the Altar Boys' Room behind the sacristy. I have my own black cassock that buttons to my ankles, and a duplicate in red for high masses; two white cotton surplices that look like extra-large starched shirts, a celluloid collar that can be wiped clean with a damp cloth, and a large white silk bow I think will look better on a Christmas gift than around my neck.

I dread setting the alarm at five-thirty a.m. to serve at the six a.m. mass. While other O'Flynns sleep, I wash my face and comb pomade jelly through my hair, parting it neatly on the left side. I pull on a white T-shirt, khaki pants and white sneakers. I bound down the stairs out on to Loring Place. The only sound is the milkman's clanging bottles.

"Hello, Séamus," he says. "Why up so early on a Saturday?"

It will sound weird if I tell him I'm on my way to church. But I can't think of another reason that won't be suspicious. I shouldn't lie because in a few minutes I'll be standing on the altar at St Nick's.

"I'm a new altar boy. This is my first mass," I say somewhat embarrassed. I certainly wouldn't want him to think I'm a *goody-goody-holy-roller* or something.

"That will keep you out of trouble," he says.

The first rays of the sun dance on top of the cobblestones. An almost empty trolley car rattles along Fordham Road.

Mr Goldstein is opening the candy store. "Up early today, Séamus," he says. "Have you come to get the paper?"

"No I'm on my way to St Nick's."

I have a sense, a wonderful feeling; I'm at a crossroad in my short, fun-filled life. I've learned about God at school and at home. Now I'll be allowed behind the communion rail where only priests preside. I'll speak in ancient Latin. I'll be in the middle of a rite almost two thousand years old.

I walk into the sacristy behind the altar and into the locker room. Dennis Morrissey from Andrews Avenue is already dressed. This is his second year as an altar boy.

"Hi Séamus. First mass this morning?" he asks. He tells me to relax. If I forget the Latin responses there's a card on the altar steps I can read from. But the priests and nuns stress the necessity of memorization.

"I've got it down, I think," I button my black cassock and pull on the white surplice.

I walk up steps to the altar and light the two candles on both sides of the sanctuary. Dennis pours the water and wine into cruets. The odor of wine makes me think of the Sweeneys and Mr McCarthy.

Seeing the interior of the church from the altar startles me. It's cavernous. Quiet. There's no music at daily mass. The rising sun is flooding light through the massive rose window spreading a rainbow of color over the main altar. A few dozen people, mostly old women, sit in the first few pews.

The celebrant is Father Kruger, the pastor. Bad luck. He's cantankerous.

Father Kruger takes a gold chalice from the safe where the unblessed wine is also stored. He places an embroidered shawl-like piece of material over the chalice.

"Ready?" he asks.

The three of us walk to the altar steps, genuflect. Father Kruger places the covered chalice on the altar. Dennis and I kneel on the steps.

"In nomine patris, et filio, et spiritu sancto....."

When it's time for the altar boys' response I wait till Dennis begins the Latin to help trigger my memory.

Just before the communion we go to a side table and take the cruets and a small towel up to Father Kruger. Dennis pours holy water over Father Kruger's outstretched fingers, which I learned is symbolic of washing sins away. I'm close to Father Kruger. His breath already smells of alcohol. I start to pour some wine into the chalice. Father Kruger grabs the cruet emptying all the wine into the golden vessel. He gives me an angry look. I don't know what's wrong. Did I make a mistake?

We turn and start down the steps. Dennis whispers: "Forgot to tell you, Séamus, Kruger's got a drinking problem. Altar boys always pour every drop of wine from the cruet into his chalice."

The drunken Sweeneys with filthy mouths had lived next door. Mr McCarthy is always tipsy. Now Father Kruger.

At communion, I hold the paten, a plate of gold with a wooden handle under the chin of each communicant. I'm to catch fragments that may fall off the host. As we move along the communion rail, Father Kruger places a circle of thin bread on each tongue. Jesus Christ is inside the wafer. Although I enjoy mystery and ritual, I find it hard to believe the wafer becomes the body and blood of Christ. But from this side of the railing I see parishioners, eyes and heads lowered, humbly waiting for Father Kruger to place the consecrated host on their tongues. They have to go to mass on Sunday under pain of sin. Yet they're here at six a.m. on Saturday. Hey, Séamus, you don't have to be here either. I am learning I really do have a soul inside me someplace. I can feel it.

A few days later I'm soaking in a warm tub listening to the Yankees and Cardinals in the last game of the World Series. It's the top of the 5th inning. Tommy Henrich homered. Joe DiMaggio flied out to center field. Charlie Keller struck out. If the Yankees take today's game they will win the series four to one. Last year they lost to St Louis one to four. I'm trying to concentrate on the game but I keep going back to the experience of my first mass as an altar boy. If I become a priest it doesn't mean I can't go to the Yankee Stadium or Polo Grounds. But I'll have to give up pleasures I'm just beginning to discover. And besides, Father Kruger doesn't seem too happy.

THE DOMINICAN NUNS at St Nick's don't have last names. They can't come to your apartment for dinner or visit their family homes ever again. A house visit may be a temptation for a Bride of Christ to return to materialism or God forbid, an old boyfriend. Nuns are clothed in yards and yards of white material that almost touches the ground. Something like the white alb the Pope wears. They have their hands tucked out of sight under a long white piece of material hanging from their necks to their black shoes. Must be hidden pockets under those folds. Their necks, ears and foreheads are covered with the same heavy material. A long black veil cascades down their backs. A giant rosary with fifteen decades of beads dangles down the left side harnessed by a black leather cincture.

An individual nun's face is all that's different, but it's still difficult to tell them apart. Glasses are the same. Rimless with square lenses, probably issued by the motherhouse in Blauvelt, New York. There doesn't seem to be any middle ground in temperament. A nun is either deliriously happy, smiling all the time, or a down-in-the-dumps grouch. One, Sister Mary Ita, looks cranky all the time. She's the school disciplinarian.

It's my turn to be whacked. Sister Helen Marie, my seventh grade teacher has marched me to the eighth grade classroom. Quietly opening the door, Sister Helen Marie asks Sister Mary Ita if she has a minute.

"Of course I do, Sister Helen," she says sweetly. "Who is it this time?"

"Séamus O'Flynn."

"Pardon me class," Sister Mary Ita says. "This will only take a moment."

Sister Helen tells me to enter the classroom. My sister Siobhan is in the class.

"Quiet, children," Sister Mary Ita scolds.

"Séamus, please put your right hand out, palm up."

She opens a desk draw and withdraws a fat, wide twenty-four inch ruler. At least it's not a yardstick. I spot the ruler's gleaming brass edge. It's about to cut a bright red line across my palm.

My sister puts her head in her hands.

Wwwhhaaackk.

"Two more," she says.

Sssmmaaackkk. Smmaackk.

My face is in flames, redder than my throbbing hand.

"Now children," Sister Mary Ita says, "let's get back to catechism to discuss the need for penance in our lives."

I TELL MY mother about the bashing I got.

"What did you do wrong?"

"We were practicing in the church for the boys' choir after lunch. I was horsing around with Danny and Sister Helen Marie told me to stop. I didn't."

"You deserved the punishment," my mother says sternly. "I must tell your father. Just hope he judges the bruising on your hand to be sufficient punishment."

"...tell your father..." Whenever my mother says my father will deal with my sisters, or me, ordinary fear becomes holy terror. It will be hours until he comes home from work. I think waiting for him should be enough punishment.

"I'll be good, I'll be good."

My father uses a belt or hairbrush. He'll have less than an hour to mete out his punishment, eat dinner, then catch the New York Central train to his other job as a handyman at the Hastings Yacht Club.

The retribution takes place in the bathroom with the door closed. My father tells me to drop my pants. I bend over and take my punishment. My sisters are outside crying. When one of them is in the hot seat I wail outside with my other sister. Sobbing, pleading children help moderate my father's punishment.

My parents tell us they were severely disciplined when they were children in Ireland. The rod was the most common means of punishment. And they told us children were often severely beaten at school.

"In fact, we're lucky," my sister says. "Mrs Curran in 2D strips her children naked. She ties their hands with rope to the showerhead. Then she whips them."

THE SCREECH OF sirens wakes everyone at 222. It's five a.m. Heads pop out of the windows of the front apartments. Police are rushing down the steps to the basement.

"I'll bet one of the McCarthys is dead," my mother says.

"Did you hear anything odd last night?" Mrs Hennessey in 3B yells up to my mother.

"I did." says Mr Fitzgerald in 4B. "I heard sobbing in the night in the alleyway."

The police go to each apartment asking what we may have heard.

"Mr McCarthy is dead," the policeman says.

I climb out on the fire escape by my parents' bedroom and watch Mr McCarthy's body being moved into a police van. Mrs McCarthy follows, in handcuffs.

"She's killed him," shouts Mr Fitzgerald to the hordes hanging out windows.

"He deserved it."

"I could hear him beating her when he was drunk," says Mrs Daly from 1D. "We live directly over their apartment. He's an evil man."

"They're Catholic and never went to mass."

"The McCarthy kids went to the public school instead of St Nick's."

The story is front page in the *Journal American*. Sheila McCarthy's left eye is bruised and almost shut. Her lip requires four stitches. She hit her husband over the head with the shovel McCarthy used to scoop the coal into the furnace. Mrs McCarthy pulled up a chair and sat watching the blood running out of her unconscious husband. When the blood stopped, she called the police.

Maureen Daly is the star witness. From 1D she often heard Mike McCarthy's threats and the sobs of Sheila McCarthy when he beat her. From her kitchen window she saw McCarthy staggering into his basement apartment. She testified he seemed to be in a perpetual state of drunkenness. Other tenants are called to testify.

The halls buzz for weeks. Shouldn't Mrs McCarthy have called the police sooner? How could she sit calmly in a chair and see his life running out on the basement's cement floor?

The jury took only an hour to deliberate. The story again makes the front page of the *Journal American*. Evidence provided by the 222 brigade proves Mike McCarthy was drunk most of the time and he had severely beaten his wife for years. Not guilty. The judge, nevertheless, admonished Sheila McCarthy for the coldhearted way she let her husband die.

"See what drink does to the Irish," my mother says.

THE CURSE OF the Irish pockmarked 222. Besides the now deceased Mr McCarthy and Mr Sweeney, guzzlers include Mrs Hanrahan in 1B, Mr Murphy 2C, Mr Fitzgerald 4B. In our small building of twenty apartments *this curse* has already caused a suicide and a murder.

My mother proudly tells us no one drinks in her Irish or American families. She says the long tradition of abstinence probably is traced back to the 1838 temperance movement. Half the population in Ireland took a pledge of moderation or total abstinence. She believes that's why the O'Learys are teetotalers.

I recall a few Thanksgivings when my mother sipped some Port wine as she cooked the turkey. We looked forward to her ten minutes of insobriety as her pearly skin broke out in red blotches and she slurred her way through the *Grace Before Meals.*

The O'Flynn side of the family imbibes, but only a *wee bit.* When my parents discuss drinking, my father points out even Jesus drank wine. My mother says thousands of years ago wine didn't contain alcohol. My father says Jesus' first miracle was turning large jugs of water into wine at the wedding feast of Cana and if it didn't contain alcohol the wedding guests wouldn't have said how wonderful it was for the host to have saved the best wine until last. My mother tells my father to be careful how he interprets the bible because the devil quotes scripture too.

"I still don't think there's alcohol in the biblical wine," my mother says.

"Well how come there are so many instances of drunkenness in the bible?" my father says.

My mother finds it difficult to believe Jesus, Mary and Joseph drank wine. She isn't completely against drinking. There's a bottle of Seagram's Seven Crown Blended Whiskey in the hall closet. For guests. My father sometimes has a ball and a beer, a shot glass of whiskey chased down with a cold Guinness.

"I work two jobs and need a pick-me-up when I come home from twelve hours work," my father explains to us. "You kids have never seen me tipsy, now have you?" True.

ELEVEN

LARRY AND FREDDIE are on base. Danny pitches the spaldine underhand. The broomstick catches the sprightly pink rubber ball propelling it over Ray's head. He chases the spaldine up cobbled-stoned Loring Place hill. I dart to today's first base, the front bumper of the Hanrahan's 1939 black Dodge roadster, glide over a Con-Edison manhole cover which is second base, touch the door handle of the Daly's 1940 dark green Buick coupe, today's third base. I want to slide into home plate like a Yankee, but it's another manhole cover.

"Three runs. That's great," the priest says.

"Doesn't happen often," I say.

He's in a black suit and white Roman collar. He waves to us and walks down the hill to Fordham Road.

"He may be from Fordham University," I say.

I'm leaving the butcher's with pigs' feet and blood pudding when he comes up to me.

"You're the boy who hit the home run up Loring Place. Good hit. How did it turn out?"

"We won," I say. "But it's not like the Yankees playing the Dodgers. We all live on Loring Place and we mix up sides. If you really want to see a rough game watch when our seventh grade team plays the seventh graders from Andrews Avenue, the next street over."

"What's your name?" the priest asks.

"Séamus O'Flynn."

"Well, Séamus. You hit a home run, and you're Irish. Good reasons to let me treat you to an egg-cream. I see you're carrying groceries. I'm sure your mother won't mind."

I know my mother will be thrilled when I tell her a priest thought enough of me to buy me a chocolate soda.

"Thank you, father. Let's go to Goldstein's Candy Store, a few steps up Fordham Road."

"I'm Father Cronin," he says.

"I know you're not from St Nick's," I say. "I know all the Augustinians at St Nick's. Are you a Jesuit from Fordham University?"

"No, Séamus, I'm from Brooklyn."

"Hello Father. Hello Séamus," Mr Goldstein says. You're not from St Nick's, are you?"

"No. Just in the neighborhood today. I saw Séamus hit a spaldine to the top of Loring Place. Thought he deserved a treat." Father Cronin gave me a hug.

"Séamus is a good boy," Mr Goldstein says. "He worked for me for two years. After school he took his baby carriage to the newspaper drop-off site under the Fordham el station. He picked up my copies of the evening *Journal American* and *Post*."

"Mr Goldstein paid me two dollars a week for a few hours work," I say.

"Now and then I threw in a free Baby Ruth," Mr Goldstein smiles.

"Tell me about your family, Séamus," Father Cronin says.

"Both my parents are from Ireland. My father works for the New York Central and I have two sisters, Sinead and Siobhan."

"I would love to meet your family, Séamus."

"I know my parents would like to meet you sometime."

"How about right now?"

"You'd have to climb up five flights of stairs."

"Séamus, I told you I'm from Brooklyn. All our parishioners live in apartments, just like you do."

I never remembered a priest in our apartment. St Nick's young curate, Father Meehan, would occasionally visit Mrs Curran on the second floor. My parents heard the Currans were having problems. My mother says the 222 rumor is the counseling Mrs Curran's getting is very personal. I know what the tittering is about, but don't believe anything's going on. Father Meehan prepared me for First Communion and stressed a mortal sin is a one-way ticket to hell.

My mother is leaning out the living room window.

"Séamus," she yells down. "Anything wrong, Séamus?"

"My mother thinks I'm in trouble because you're with me, father," I say. "Everything's O.K., mom. We're coming up."

The hallways of 222 are empty. I hoped someone would see me walking up the stairs with a priest.

My mother meets us at the door.

"Mrs O'Flynn, I'm Father Cronin. I had to meet Séamus' parents. He's such a wonderful, young Catholic gentleman. You must be very proud."

"We're delighted you're paying us a visit, father. My husband is coming up the stairs behind you. We hope you can join us for pickled pig's feet and cabbage. A real delicacy in the old sod."

"Sorry. I'm just paying my respects. I can only stay a few minutes. I have a long subway ride to Brooklyn. A cup of tea would be wonderful."

"Where did Séamus learn to hit the ball like that," Father Cronin asks my father. "Were you a hurler as a lad?"

"I was for the first few years after coming to New York. The last time I played, I got cocked over the eye. Kit, seeing the blood all over my face made me quit. Now it's only horseshoes and bowling. Did Séamus tell you he's an altar boy and also sings in the boys' choir?"

"It doesn't surprise me," Father Cronin says. "Séamus come sit with me."

Father Cronin sat in an armchair. He motions to me to sit on one of his knees. He pulls me close. He crosses his left leg in front of me. I feel awkward. It's a long time since I sat on anyone's lap.

My mother and father are glowing.

"Do you ever go to Gaelic Park to the hurling matches?" Father Cronin asks my father.

"We go about twice a month. It's a body-bruising game. Kit doesn't like the blood and broken bones."

Father Cronin's hand eases into my right pocket. I look at my parents sitting comfortably on the couch. My father is describing a goal the Galway team scored last week. Father Cronin pushes my pocket lining beneath my underwear and cups my balls in his hand.

"What team was Galway playing?" Father Cronin asks.

Séamus...jump up right now. His left arm has me in a tight grip while his right hand is out of my parents' view. Why aren't they saying anything?

Oh my god. Oh, no. What's he doing? Please, God, don't let him touch me like this.

My mother is telling Father Cronin how much women hate Irish hurling. "All those young men getting bashed with the hurley stick. They just about kill each other. There's really no sport in it. Their wives suffer the most."

Now his big hand's got hold of everything.

I try to pull his hand out of my pocket but I can't. I see the fire escape behind my father. I've been afraid someone would climb up from the street and get me. And my parents always said no one would want you.

"How do you like the way the Augustinians run St Nick's," Father Cronin asks lifting his crossed leg higher.

This is going on in our living room. Right before my parents' eyes. They're gloating over him. I'm feeling sick.

Father Cronin begins to tremble. His voice cracks.

"Are you alright, father?" my mother asks.

"Oh, just something I had for lunch," he says, sliding his hand out of my pocket.

"Well, Father Cronin, I know it's not the tea. You haven't touched your cup."

TWELVE

In August 1937, Gregory and his brother Sonny were driving in a 1935 Dodge four-door sedan on U.S. Highway One through Connecticut. A drunk driver coming in the opposite direction jumped lanes. Uncle Sonny was killed instantly. Now two of my mother's brothers have been killed in accidents in their adopted country. Gregory was in critical condition for months.

"Maybe we should have stayed in Cork," my mother writes to her mother. "We would still have Harry and Sonny."

My mother says, "Your grandmother is almost four thousand miles away, and I can hear her keening. I really can."

UNCLE GREGORY JOINED the Army a few weeks after Pearl Harbor. For two years he has been making requests to go overseas but the brass say they need him at Fort Barancas in Pensacola, Florida. My mother thinks he may be too old at thirty-three to go into combat. She seems to be happy his requests are turned down. The Army recognizes his considerable writing talents. Uncle Gregory is working in communications and publications. The Army has been publishing poems he writes about infantrymen. He's just been promoted to First Sergeant. Uncle Gregory is my mother's youngest brother. He was the Cork County champion in bicycle racing in the one, three and five mile races. My mother says his handsome face may have been sculpted by the great winds blowing west from the Atlantic across Roaringwater Bay to the family farm in Skibbereen. He has a jutting chin and a long nose with wide flaring nostrils. His ears look like they had been blown back from his face by a piercing gale. He combs his pomaded light brown hair straight back into deep narrow furrows. His enormous mouth is always smiling since he's constantly rejoicing about his new life in America.

"I'm right at home on the Island of Manhattan," he said. "I left the Island of Ireland where my home town of Skibbereen has only two thousand people. In New York there are four million. And one million are from the old sod. Just think of the unlimited supply of beautiful Irish lasses waiting to meet me," he chuckles.

Gregory wasn't always so upbeat my mother says. He had arrived in the spring of 1929 and found work immediately constructing apartment buildings along Fifth Avenue. In the fall, the stock market crashed and the Great Depression began. He was laid off. But he saw the bright side. "Millions lost every cent they had," Uncle Gregory told me, "but I came out O.K. because I didn't even have a penny to lose."

Gregory told us about the Irish Republican Army. After World War I when he was eleven he was dragged out of bed in the middle of the night by the English Black and Tans. They were searching for his older brother Dick who was a secret member of the IRA. My father told Gregory about his daredevil deeds for the IRA running messages on his bicycle for K Company, Second Battalion, Third Cork Brigade. For Irish boys it seems there had to be a scuffle with the Black and Tans to pass into manhood.

A year before he emigrated, a letter from Uncle Gregory included a new poem he had written, THE BRAVE I.R.A. My father had the poem set in type and framed. It hangs in our living room.

The Saxon's been with us
Each night and day
He's tortured, he's plundered
He's hanged and he's hunted
But he NEVER could conquer
The brave I.R.A.

The spirit of freedom
Still shines like a beacon
With the help of our friends
in the great U.S.A.

Let England start heeding
and her exit start speeding
There's no place for her here
We'll wipe out the border
and establish true order
With a peace that is just
And our flags in array
With her Paras and Tommies
Her guns and her tanks
She's failed to conquer
The brave I.R.A.

From Cork up to Derry
From Antrim to Kerry
Through Wexford, Tipp'rary
and back to Tyrone
There'll be joy 'mongst our people
in each church, 'neath each steeple
And the blessings of God
Will reign in our isle
Then we'll march down the years
No more distrust or fears
When John Bull we've banished
With his chains in decay
To rule us he tried
As he murdered and spied
But he NEVER could conquer
The brave I.R.A.

—Gregory O'Leary

SEVEN HUNDRED YEARS of suffering in Ireland have produced some good Uncle Gregory says. Since there were no jobs for Irishmen in their own land, millions emigrated to America.

Uncle Gregory is also a tenor. He sang in pubs and at dances in Cork. He soon became known in New York's Irish community. The most celebrated Irish tenor, Dennis Day, was a star on Jack Benny's radio show. Dennis was a judge at a Feis in Brooklyn where my uncle won first prize for his rendition of *Irish Rebel's Grave*. Dennis Day helped my uncle get a recording contract with Decca Records. My uncle told us Day's real name was Owen Patrick Eugene McNulty. He was born in the Bronx and went to Manhattan College. My uncle says one day he'll be better known than Dennis Day because he's a tenor with a real Irish brogue.

For Uncle Gregory's first record, *A Mother's Love Is A Blessing*, Decca paired him with their leading Irish soprano Josephine Beirne. It sold over half a million records. Decca contracted for a second record with the duo singing *Faithful Soldier Boy*. "We have our very own Nelson Eddy and Jeanette McDonald," my father says.

Uncle Gregory bursts into our apartment in high spirits. He picks me up and spins me around holding one arm and leg. He tosses Sinead so high he breaks a ceiling fixture in the living room. During dinner my mother plays his records on the wind-up Victrola. After finishing my mother's apple pie Uncle Gregory is delighted to sing along with his recording.

As an Irish boy was leaving
Leaving his native home
Crossing the broad Atlantic
Once more he wished to roam
And as he was leaving his mother
And walking all the day
He threw his arms around his head
And these were the words he said:
A mother's love is a blessing
No matter where you roam
Keep her while she's living
You'll miss her when she's gone
Love her as in childhood
Tho' feeble old and gray
For you'll never miss a mother's love
'Till she is buried beneath the clay.

My mother's eyes mist and look faraway. Is she sad because Uncle Gregory hasn't seen his mother since 1929? Is it her own yearning? She puts her arm around Sinead and gives loving winks to Siobhan and me.

Uncle Gregory made thirty records for Decca. They play on New York's Irish radio stations. The halls of 222 buzz when the famous Irish tenor recording star visits the O'Flynns. On Saturdays and Sundays my parents have the

Irish stations on all day and hear Uncle Gregory's lilting songs. In summer when windows are open, his songs echo in the alleyway.

My uncle is singing on WPOW about the O'Leary's old hometown of Skibbereen. My mother says *Old Skibbereen* was written after the Irish potato famine in the mid-eighteen hundreds when almost one million died of starvation and another million emigrated to America.

Oh, son I loved my native land
With energy and pride
Till a blight came o're my crops
My sheep, my cattle died
My rent and taxes were too high
I could not them redeem
And that's the cruel reason
I left old Skibbereen.

Oh, well do I remember
The bleak December day
The landlord and the sheriff came
To drive us all away
They set my roof on fire
With cursed English spleen
And that's another reason
That I left old Skibbereen

Oh, father dear, the day may come
When in answer to the call
Each Irishman, with feeling stern
Will rally one and all
I'll be the man to lead the van
Beneath the flag of green
When loud and high we'll raise the cry
—REMEMBER SKIBBEREEN.

THIRTEEN

This war is grotesque.

A SLIP OF THE LIP, MAY SINK A SHIP...LOOSE TALK COSTS LIVES...BUY WAR BONDS...DON'T TALK CHUM, CHEW TOPPS GUM.

This war is monstrous.

Every Saturday at the Paradise Theater I see Japs and Germans in newsreels shooting, bayoneting, bombing. I started saving front pages of the *New York Daily Mirror* the day after Pearl Harbor, ROOSEVELT DECLARES WAR. Now I have a draw full of World War II headlines in thick black letters. I see Hollywood movies with Japanese Zero pilots dive-bombing our ships. Swastikered Nazis in Junka Stukas shooting down British Spitfires. Goosestepping German troops enslaving the whole world.

While I should be listening to Sister Helen Marie at school I doodle on scraps of paper. Before the war I drew my own fantasy rockets spouting fire on their way to Mars and the moon. Now I draw Stukas and Zeros being chased by American P-47 Thunderbolts with guns blazing. From the Thunderbolt's guns I sketch a dotted line - - - - - - - - - of deadly bullets- - - - - - tearing into Jap and Nazi fighter planes. In penmanship class the nuns make us draw endless intertwined circles across lined paper to make our handwriting as beautiful as theirs. Now I draw these endless circles to mark the path the Jap and German planes take as they fall from the sky crashing into the Atlantic and Pacific Oceans, downed by my P-47 pencil drawing. I've come up with my own secret weapon, deadlier than Thunderbolts. I've redesigned my drawing of the pre-war rocket ship by adding a large glass bubble underneath to hold gunners and the bombardier. With this extra fighting power, I can really do a job on the axis planes, every day, right here on my school desk.

I hate Japs more than the Germans. Kamikaze pilots with tooth-filled-yellow-ear-to-yellow-ear grins committing suicide for Japan diving into our battleships. One Jap life sinks an American ship and kills hundreds of American young men.

THE YANKEES ARE helping the war effort. Bring a can of leftover cooking fat, or five pounds of newspapers and you get into Yankee Stadium free. I ring doorbells on Loring Place asking for bacon grease and newspapers. I melt the collected meat drippings in my mother's stew pot and pour the gross mixture into Maxwell House coffee cans. Now I don't have to pay to watch Joe DiMaggio play. I feel very patriotic at the same time. Joe was also very patriotic. He enlisted in the army in 1943.

The nuns suggest another way for us to help. Soldiers and sailors are lonely. St Nick's students could adopt a serviceman. I sent a note to Uncle Gregory at Fort Barancas asking if I could write to him. He said a friend of his, Corporal Godfrey Beatty in his battalion, only receives an occasional letter from his sister in Brooklyn. He would welcome a pen pal. In a few weeks Godfrey is shipped to the European Theater. Now I send my letter to an Army P.O. box in New York and it's forwarded to him somewhere in the European Theater. In school after the Pledge of Allegiance to the Flag, we pray for our servicemen. I tell Godfrey about the movies I've seen and how I went to Ebbets Field to watch his favorite team. Bummer, the Redskins beat the Dodgers, third loss in a row.

Godfrey can't tell me where he is but does relate stories of his duty as an observer. When he spots an enemy submarine or ship from a watchtower, *flashflashflash* is his message. When I read in the paper a German battleship is sunk I wonder if Godfrey's flashing light located the enemy ship. Godfrey says he is going to take me to Radio City Music Hall when this damn war is over. He says to keep those prayers coming my way.

APARTMENT RENTS ARE frozen in July, 1943. My parents are very happy. "The landlord's being *japped* this time," my father says. "Even if there wasn't a war going on he shouldn't raise rents at 222 since he has been hiring lousy Irish drunks who don't keep the building clean."

Rationing begins. The list gets bigger; meat, butter, sugar, fats, oils, coffee, canned foods, shoes and gasoline. At Safeway my mother counts out her dollars and also carefully tears out the perforated rationing coupons. For dinner my mother bakes, fries, mixes it with macaroni, chops it in salad, but it still tastes like SPAM. I can have half a teaspoon of sugar for Rice Krispies. *Snap-crackle-pop* doesn't taste the same.

We are not cranky when mock air raids are held. In fact, it's exciting. The sirens sound, the city goes black. We pull down the shades and sit in our dark living room listening to the radio. My parents say the odds are slim New York will be attacked like London is being bombarded. My mother is grateful Ireland is a neutral country even though the war is raging in England a few miles across the Irish Sea. My three grandparents in Ireland, aunts, uncles and cousins I have never met, seem to be safe.

When it's dark, Danny becomes *Army Air Boy* and I'm *The Fighting Flag* stealing through the shadows along Loring Place. Danny puts on khaki pants and shirt and his brother's seaman's cap with two gold stars. I'm dressed in an old red knit cap, blue pants, white shirt and wear a large American flag as a cape. Our guns are made from the sawed off corners of orange crates. A rubber band is nailed to the front and stretched back to hold a small square of cardboard or old linoleum. After climbing a tree at DeVoe Park we wait for the enemy.

"I see two Japs coming," Danny says.

We fire our pistols.

"Now there are two Nazi heads peering out of that tank."

We let them have it.

Out of ammunition, we say we're doing our part in the war getting rid of imaginary Japs and Germans. We wish the enemy bodies were real.

WE ARE ABOUT to have The Battle For University Heights. A messenger on a roller skate scooter from Andrews Avenue presents a note to Larry Nolan, ringleader of Loring Place:

ANDREWS AVENUE CHALLENGES LORING PLACE

TO A DUEL

SATURDAY, SEPTEMBER 11, 1943

AT SCULL ROCK

11:00 A.M.

WEAPONS: WOOD SWORDS

BE THERE, YOU COWARDS

"I think they've seen too many war movies," Larry says. "We have no differences with Andrews Avenue. We all go to St Nick's."

"If we don't show up, they automatically win," says Danny.

"Get as many orange crates as we can find," says Ray.

The longest pieces of wood formed the shaft, whittled to a sharp point. The handle is tightly wrapped with clothesline.

The battleground is Scull Rock, a grassy hill across the street from the Bronx Campus of New York University. For as long as I can remember a black and white scull and cross bones with red eyes has been painted on the huge glacial boulder.

The gang from Andrews Avenue is waiting on one side of the rock. Loring Place is on the other.

To get us fighting mad, Larry tells us Italy just surrendered this week and declared war on Germany. Today we are Italian soldiers and Andrews Avenue are Nazis.

Nolan challenges the ringleader of Andrews Avenue, Tommy Connolly to step up on the rock. The war game begins.

"It's a fight to the death," McGlynn says.

"Let's get those Nazis sympathizers," says Larry.

I thought this battle was going to be friendly.

Connolly let's out a whoop circling his sword over his head. "You're dead, Nolan." He brings his weapon down hard. Nolan swings his sword underneath. Connolly loses his footing.

"Give it to him, Tommy. They're calling us Nazis."

"We're calling you *stinking* Nazis."

"Let's get these nuns' pets." Andrews Avenue rushes us.

"Let's see their sculls."

The warriors are scrapping on the rock. Swords splinter from furious blows.

"Ohhhh," screams Freddy whose arm crashes against a jagged chunk of Scull Rock. Bone tears through his skin.

"Stop. Stop fighting," Larry yells. "His arm is broken. Who did it? Who?"

Freddy is yelling in pain on Scull Rock surrounded by the ragged, bruised boys of University Heights.

"I'm sorry, Freddy," Tommy Connolly says. "This started out as a prank. We're all friends, not enemies. It's your fault Larry. You called us Nazis."

THE FOLLOWING WEEK, we experienced the real World War II. Wounded soldiers and sailors at Kingsbridge Veterans Hospital. We responded to the request at St Nick's for volunteers. We were not prepared for our first encounter with two soldiers waiting to play poker. I was introduced to Private First Class Terry Swenson who had lost most fingers on both hands. I shook what was left of his right hand. "You'll be my hands, Séamus," he says, "until the docs here can figure out a way to make me whole again."

After a spirited game of poker Terry asks me to help him write a letter to his parents in Boston. He tells them he's feeling fine and looks forward to coming home soon. He says he'll enroll in college as soon as everything's working again. He tells them it's great having a second pair of hands whose name is Séamus. I'm twelve. He's nineteen.

THE TOPIC IN religion class is Confirmation, the next step in our continuing development as Soldiers of Christ. Sister Helen Marie tells us we have already received three of the seven sacraments of the church, Baptism, Confession and First Holy Communion. In a month we'll commit to the fourth, Confirmation. Sister Helen Marie says we'll wait a long time to receive the last three sacraments. Holy Orders is only available to men who become celibate priests. Matrimony you already know about she says since your parents are married sacramentally in the Church.

"While I hope it will be fifty or sixty years before you partake of the seventh sacrament, Extreme Unction for the dying, you don't know the day or the hour the Lord will call you," Sister Helen Marie says. "You better be ready when He comes. If you're not, and a priest is nearby he can hear your confession and give you the last sacrament. Even if you've sinned all your life, you're saved at the end if you're near a priest. That's why there are now so many chaplains on the front lines with our boys in Europe and the South Pacific."

It looks like the rest of my life is a flip of a coin. Heads or tails? Will I be in the state of grace at the end? If not, the only way to be saved is to have a priest close at hand. I could have died many times in my short life. If Mr McCarthy had shoved me into the apartment furnace, if my head was crushed on Scull Rock, if Mr Sweeney's bullet tore through my headboard and I died instantly. How would I be saved from hell since a priest wouldn't have been in that spooky basement as McCarthy was finishing me off?

SISTER HELEN MARIE told us we had to select an additional name for Confirmation. Bishop O'Malley, one of the rectors of St Patrick's Cathedral in Manhattan, will come to St Nicholas Church to confirm us. He'll dip his fingers into chrism, a mixture of pure olive oil and an aromatic gum resin from trees, and anoint us with the sign of the cross on our forehead. Then he'll call us by our Confirmation name.

For homework, Sister Helen Marie says to discuss saints' names with our parents. Write a short story about the saint you've chosen and tell how you'll go about imitating the saint's virtues.

I was surprised to find a number of books about saints in the Kingsbridge Public Library. I thought only Catholics were interested in angels and saints. When I learned about St Patrick and his accomplishments I decided to take his name. We read our Confirmation Composition in front of the class:

For my new Confirmation name I'm taking Patrick. These are the reasons: my father's name is Patrick, I like marching in the St

Patrick's Day parade every year, I drop into St Patrick's Cathedral on Fifth Avenue to look up at its Gothic beauty and to see the statue of Patrick stepping on snakes, and finally Patrick is the most Irish name of all, besides Séamus.

My father told me Saint Patrick was one hundred percent Irish. I was surprised to learn Patrick was actually British. He was born in 390 and lived until he was 71. When he was 16, Irish pirates captured him. He was sold as a slave and took care of his master's cattle in County Antrim. For six years he was always cold and hungry. He began to recall the Christian faith of his boyhood and started to pray. In his manuscript CONFESSION he wrote he was "humbled by hunger and nakedness."

Patrick escaped to France and studied four years with St Martin of Tours and then fourteen years with St Germanus of Auxerre. After a vision he was convinced he should go back to convert all the barbarians in Ireland.

Many miracles are attributed to St Patrick. I'm amazed he could drive all the snakes in Ireland into the sea. Too bad he's not around today to drive all the Japs and Germans out of the lands they have no right to be in.

Once St Patrick learned a man had robbed a sheep and ate it. He asked the man to come forward and confess. No one responded. The Saint asked God to have the sheep speak in the belly of the thief. "Baaa, baaa," the sheep bleated. Everyone said they would never steal again, at least when St Patrick was in the neighborhood.

St Patrick used the shamrock to teach the Irish about the three persons of the Trinity. Every year my relatives in Cork send clumps of shamrock from their farms for St Patrick's Day. Even though it's dried and dead looking we wear it on our lapels in the parade. When I march by St Patrick's Cathedral wearing my shamrock from the Old Sod, I realize I'm an American boy, but like the shamrock, I too have deep roots across the sea.

St Patrick demonstrates to me the power one person has if they're committed to an ideal. What he began 1,500 years ago continues today. When I take Patrick's name for Confirmation I will try to remember the rest of my life what perseverance can accomplish.

A week later, my forehead running with holy oily chrism, the bishop turned me into a new person, Séamus William Patrick O'Flynn.

"You're still plain ol' Séamus to me," my sister Siobhan says.

FOURTEEN

Boys in St Nick's elementary school lionize boys in the high school. Voices change, you're no longer mistaken for a girl on the phone. More hair appears, everywhere. Girls in elementary school titter when they talk about high school boys. Especially the varsity basketball team.

St Nick's gym is also a hall used for school meetings and extra masses. None of the nearby parishes has a real gymnasium. Only public schools can afford such luxury. Basketball backboards are lowered from the ceilings on pulleys. Metal folding chairs are jammed into every space and lined-up a fraction of an inch from the court lines. Airborne sweaty athletes often crash into the crowd. Spectators throw up their arms in unison so the spiraling player can land on a human cushion.

When St Nick's varsity comes into the gym, Father Kruger grabs the microphone and announces the team: "Center is Joe Luna, guards are Tom Maguire and Pat Riley, forwards are Eddie Madden and Pete McGrath." The low ceiling in the gym makes the hullabaloo louder than nearby Yankee Stadium.

Father Walker, pastor of St Peter's, takes the microphone. "Now let's hear it for St Peter's Panthers, the reigning Bronx champions of the Catholic Youth Organization." Cat calls. Bronx cheers.

Father Kruger leads the varsity team in prayer. They put their hands on top of his. "Lord Jesus Christ, I ask you to bless these gallant young men who represent all of us at St Nick's. Please let it be your will tonight for St Nick's to go on to victory. We implore you, give our team strength, speed and fortitude. We ask your blessing, in the name of the Father, Son and Holy Ghost. Amen." The team holds onto Father Kruger's arms soaking in his mystical powers.

Across the hall, Father Walker has his team in a huddle. With his eyes on heaven he implores: "Gird the loins of these men of St Peter's Panthers so they can continue their unbeaten record."

St Peter's sinks the first basket. Shouting and hooting. The two Bronx pastors are creating a dilemma for the three persons of the Holy Trinity. The eager and demanding supplications of Father Kruger and Father Walker have been received in heaven. Five young men from St Nick's and five from St Peter's are battling like Christian soldiers of old. In religion class we're told zealous prayers are always answered. It's like Solomon's predicament. Each woman claims the baby in question is hers.

It's only when Solomon picks up his sword and says the way to solve the problem is to give each woman half a baby. The real mother cries out she doesn't want the baby. Give it to her. Solomon easily spots the real mother. Perhaps the real St Peter and St Nicholas have been called into the Heavenly Chamber. "See your namesakes battling it out down there. They both sent incantations up here asking to win this game. Every Friday night all over New York City, fifty Catholic high school basketball teams are pitted against each other and petitioning for Divine Intervention. How is Solomon going to straighten out this problem tonight....?" While I'm daydreaming, a ball smashes into my face.

"Where were you?" Danny chuckles.

"Do you believe God answers all prayers?" I ask.

"Of course I don't. Where did you get that idea?"

"Right here at St Nick's."

"This is not the time to get philosophical. We're behind twelve points and Father Kruger is going to have a stroke. He keeps yelling at the ref telling him he's blind. I think he's going to whip off his great black belt and hang the ref."

"That's what I'm talking about. Kruger and Walker storm heaven with prayers to win. But it look's like we're going to lose. That means God didn't answer our prayers."

St Nick's loses by one basket. St Peter's whoops it up. Father Kruger flings his metal folding chair at the referee. St Nick's students follow the pastor's lead.

"You're blind," Father Kruger wails at the referee. "McGrath was fouled. That's why he missed the basket."

"The game's been won fair and square by St Peter's. Sit down Father."

"I'll have you run out of the Catholic Youth Organization," Father Kruger says.

"You've created pandemonium," the ref yells at the pastor. "I'm reporting you to the Archdiocesan office first thing Monday morning."

Perhaps the pastor had too much wine with dinner. Father Kelly puts his arm around Father Kruger and calms him down. He apologizes to the referee and says Father Kruger isn't feeling all that well today.

The teams go to the locker rooms, chairs are folded and put under the stage. Lights are dimmed for the high school inter-parish dance. Frank Sinatra croons *What Is This Thing Called Love?*

JOHNNY CHRISTIE IS the bully of St Nick's. Johnny looks like a punch-drunk boxer. Wiry curly hair and a nose that looks like it has been broken and re-set off-center. He looks something like John L. Sullivan the heavyweight Irish-American boxer, but pint-sized. He and three of his cronies prowl Loring Place looking for trouble. This is our street. He belongs on University Avenue and should stay there.

"Hey skinny" he yells at me sitting on the stoop of 222 playing *pick-up-sticks* with Danny and Larry. "Want to know what you should do with those sticks?"

Then he directs his wrath at Larry who's a bit on the pudgy side. "Fatso, that stick game is for girls. Maybe you're a girl under all those rolls of fat."

"Fat and skinny had a race, all around the pillow case...."

"Take off Johnny," I say.

"Who's going to make me? A little Leprechaun like you, O'Flynn?"

I get off the stoop and he pushes me against the building. I'm a head over him. I wonder if I can take him. I'm a year older. But Johnny's right, I'm scrawny. I know I'm going to have to defend myself. I see hooligans in the movies. Here's Johnny Christie, a living, breathing reincarnation from The Dead End Kids snorting at me on peaceful Loring Place.

"Whew." My knees wither. Johnny's arm is pressed against my throat. My head is pinned down on the sidewalk. I spot Joan O'Rourke in 3A peering out her living room window. Her sweet angelic face gives me special power. My hand shoots under Tommy's neck and my knee hits him in the stomach.

Now I'm on top of the hooligan. He tries to wrap his leg around my neck to snap me off, but his short legs can't reach me. I push both his arms over his head and hold them tightly to the cement.

"Say uncle," I demand.

"What the hell are you squawking about," Johnny cries. "Get off me."

"Stay off Loring Place you bully."

"I can go where I want and no Loring Leprechaun can tell me different."

"Well, I'm telling you to stay away from our territory."

Christie got up and starts walking down the hill with his buddies.

"This is not the last of it, O'Flynn. My brother Jimmy will be back and beat the crap out of you and your *weird pick-up-sticks friends*."

"I didn't think you could pin him down like that," Larry says.

"I may be skinny but bet I weigh the same as Johnny. I've got all my weight like my dad, in my butt and these thick Irish legs."

"Do you think his brother will come back?" Danny asks.

"Danny, you know Jimmy Christie. He's a gentle-man. Johnny is the bully of St Nick's."

"Where did that sudden burst of energy come from Séamus," Larry asks.

"When my head was on the sidewalk I saw Joan O'Rourke peering out her window. I could tell she was routing for me."

That afternoon I sent a coupon to Charles Atlas. I saw his advertisements in newspapers and magazines. There's a cartoon story of a skinny guy trying to talk to two bathing beauties. Another guy with huge muscles tells him to take off. He walks away dejected. He needs a new powerful body. He sends off his coupon to Charles Atlas and a few months later he's been transformed into a bruiser. Just in case Johnny Christie comes back I better be ready. I wait anxiously for my copy of *"The Charles Atlas Way to Big Muscles."* It never comes. I lied on the coupon I was eighteen. When the salesman called, my mother told him I was only twelve.

FIFTEEN

Her soft flesh rubs against my corduroy knickers in an elevator plunging toward the lobby of the Empire State Building.

On the 86th floor observation deck I noticed her stretching over the limestone wall for a better view of Fifth Avenue below. Her skirt eased up the back of her thin legs. A strong wind sailed through her brown hair. She saw me staring and looked away. Her eyes are brown too. I glowed brighter than the lights illuminating the Empire State. She smiles. I know that face is burned into my memory for all time.

Her father intrudes: "Time to go, Colleen. The elevator's going down." I follow as if his command is directed at me.

"You've got good taste," Danny whispers. "With a name like that I'll bet she's Irish."

The elevator cab shakes back and forth, side to side. She's off-balance and falls against me. I move closer. In a few moments she'll be gone. Why don't you ask her who she is?

"Yuummm," Danny whispers in my ear.

I say with as much authority as I can muster, "Interesting isn't it Danny, in winter snowflakes near the Empire State Building fall *up* instead of down." Colleen smiles.

I try again. "In high winds the building sways more than twenty feet from side to side."

"That's not true," the elevator man snaps. "There's only a three inch sway off the building's axis."

The elevator doors open. Her father takes her arm. They disappear into the vast marble lobby.

"Séamus, your face is still flushed," Danny says.

"In New York your body's always being rammed into perfect strangers. Colleen knew what she was doing. She didn't pull away from me. Colleen rubbed me the right way and I liked it."

Now and then I think about the priesthood. One day I think it's a good idea. The next day I know that's not the life I want. My parents keep reminding the O'Flynns have never given a boy or girl to the church. After I graduate, I'll be thirteen, the age I could enter the Augustinian seminary in Philadelphia. Today, Colleen, you may never know you helped me make a final decision. The priesthood is not for me. I'm going on to high school here at St Nick's.

SINCE BROWN-EYED, brown-haired Colleen Of-The-Empire-State has vanished who knows where, I decide to invite Joan O'Rourke to go with me to St Nicholas School's outing to Bear Mountain. This is the first year eighth graders are bringing dates on the annual Dayliner cruise up the Hudson River. Joan lives in 3A two floors below me at 222 Loring Place.

I pick up the telephone and for a dry run I say *hello...hello... hello* to be certain my voice is working so I can speak unruffled. I dial her number but hang up before she answers. This is, after all, the first time I'm going to ask a girl for an official date. I have to do it right.

I've heard my older sister turn down Joe Luna because my mother doesn't think she should date an Italian. "But mother," my sister shrieks, "his parents are immigrants just like you and daddy."

"They really don't speak the King's English like we do," my mother says. "And there's the smell of garlic. And when you marry one, you marry the whole family."

"Mom," my sister cried, "I'm only fifteen. Who's talking about marriage? Joe is the star of St Nick's basketball team."

"I said no," my mother says. "That's final."

When Joe calls my sister, she handles him delicately, but turns him down. I notice she also tells lies to other boys who call. "I'm busy that night," she'll say, or "I'm behind on my school reports so I can't go anywhere for a few weeks."

Rejection. The guy on the other end of my sister's line must feel crappy. I certainly don't want to hit bottom on my first call for a date. So I won't be at a loss for words, I'll write out a full script. I like to write anyhow. My sister is taking typing in high school and we have a Royal portable typewriter.

SCRIPT ASKING FOR A DATE

ME: *Hello Joan. This is Séamus O'Flynn.*

JOAN; (Possible responses she can give)

1. *Oh, hello, Séamus,*

or

2. *Whoooo......?*

ME: *Séamus. Séamus O'Flynn. I'm in your class at St Nick's.*

I live above in apartment 5A.

JOAN: *Oh,* (Long pause) *How are you Séamus?*

ME: (You'll be nervous. Don't let your voice show it.)

Just fine. I was looking out the window half an hour

ago and saw you coming up the hill. You had your

cheerleader's outfit on. How often do you practice?

JOAN: (Hopefully she will talk for a minute or so....)

ME: (At the next lull in conversation)

Our basketball team has a great record this year.......

(Keep talking about basketball...)

(Is she coldhearted, or does she sound friendly?)

If she's cold, try these topics:

1. The scream in the alleyway last night...

2. Our new scary super at 222...

3. The number of times Sister Mary Ita used her ruler to bash kids from our class.

(If she's warmed up–ASK HER NOW YOU COWARD.)

ME: *NEXT WEEK, JOAN, IS THE SCHOOL TRIP TO*

BEAR MOUNTAIN. I'M WONDERING IF YOU

WOULD LIKE TO GO WITH ME.

(Say NO MORE....now it's her turn.)

JOAN: (Possible responses she can give:)

1. I already have a date...

2. I'm not going on the boat ride...

3. Yes...

ME: If yes, no more script needed.

If no, say: "I'll call you again sometime."

I practiced out loud a few times. Joan has always been nice to me. Says hello when we pass each other in 222 and in class. Danced with me once after the basketball game. I think she likes me. Good thinking. Pump yourself up. NOW PICK UP

THE PHONE. She's just two floors below you right now. She may even be waiting for you to call.

Her phone is ringing. Relax. Get ready to read the script.

"Hello." Oh, no, it's not Joan. It's her older brother. The one with the deep voice. The one on the high school debate team. The baseball star. My script doesn't tell me what to say. Stupid. Just ask if she's home.

"Hello," my voice trembles. I hope he hasn't noticed. "Tom, this is Séamus O'Flynn. You know. Upstairs. The fifth floor." My voice cracks. "Is Joan home?"

"Joan it's for you. The fifth floor is calling."

"Séamus," Joan says. "How nice of you to call. I was just thinking about the school boat ride to Bear Mountain next week." Oh my god, she's not following my script. She's already mentioning the boat ride. That's supposed to be my question. I run my finger down the script looking for the words I'm supposed to say.

"I'm wondering if you would like to go with me to Bear Mountain, Joan?"

"I would love to Séamus. Seems like everyone in the eighth grade is getting a date."

We're the same age, but Joan already looks like a senior in high school. She's blond. My sister says it comes from a Peroxide bottle. Her roots are black. Actually she isn't blond. She's straw, a golden color. She must have sun bathed on the roof because she already has a slight tan. I don't know why I always notice her legs, stare at them. This is what good legs must be about. I don't know what's right about them, except they're smooth and they belong on an older woman, like an eighteen year old. She wears a lot of white blouses and billowing skirts.

The prepared script is a big success. Even though I had to jump to the bottom of the page right off, I continued my first phone conversation with Joan using the subjects I had listed. Next time I'll have to revise my script because Joan's mother, father, sister or brother could answer the phone. I should try to talk to them for a moment. About the weather, or something funny about the apartment building. A rehearsal script helps me relax.

I feel especially good when I see Joan, and feel even better when we spend time together. She understands me more than my parents or sisters. We don't even have to say much to each other. It isn't sexual. At least I don't think it is. She's angelic. The guys start to give it to me when they spot us walking through the park.

It's impossible to be alone with Joan. Mothers in 222 are always home. No one has a job. No one seems to ever leave the neighborhood, except to go to a movie now and then or in the summer to Rockaway Beach or Coney Island. When

I'm in her apartment we sit in the living room. I don't like going to 3A when her father's there. He peers at me over his newspaper. Her mother walks me to the door to be certain I'm leaving. We know we're being watched all the time. Nuns at school during the day, and by our parents the rest of the time. The only time I have courage to put my arm around Joan is at the Saturday matinee. Our parents don't know we meet at the Lowe's Paradise Theater. Nothing happens of course. I slide my arm around the back of her seat and inch it closer as the movie progresses. I don't feel I have the right to actually have my hand on her arm. Once in a while my hand does brush her. She doesn't object. Another place we feel close is in the apartment's small lobby, under the stairs by the mailboxes. We only have a few seconds because she has to ring her apartment buzzer when we enter the building. She always does as she's told. Anyhow, we're sure her mother is peeking out the window waiting for us to start up Loring Place. Under the stairs we hold each other for a few moments and I kiss her gently. She responds as best she can considering our time restraints and her mother on the third floor landing coughing like crazy so we can hear her.

"J-O-A-NNNNN," her mother's voice comes down the stairwell. *"It's getting LATE."*

A MONTH BEFORE graduation Joan gets bad news. Her family will be moving at the end of the month. Another family has already put a deposit on their apartment. Why is she moving so suddenly? Why doesn't she know where she's going? She won't talk to me.

A few days later my father notices a small item in the *Journal American*. Her father is suspected of taking large amount of cash from a downtown branch of the Bank of New York and Trust Company. Mr O'Rourke is one of the few men at 222 who wear a suit to work. He graduated from high school in Dublin before coming to America. He's been let go. A trial is pending.

I stop Joan on the way to school and tell her I'm sorry. She starts to cry. "We're moving in a week. I think we're going way out on Long Island somewhere. My mother's sister lives in Montauk. It's as far away as we can possibly go without my parents going all the way back to Ireland."

In a few days she'll be gone. I've never had this feeling before. Empty. Lonely. When I think of her apartment being vacant I have to catch my breath. It's like having a bronchitis attack.

I have a brilliant idea. Joan says it's crazy. If we're caught I'll be in serious trouble. But the rendezvous is set tonight at eleven.

We check to be certain our dumbwaiter doors are left unlocked. When everyone in my apartment is asleep, I quietly go to the kitchen. From the window I can see all the lights are out in the O'Rourke's apartment too. I've stationed the dumbwaiter on the fifth floor. I squeeze into the small space and wrap the pulley line around my hand. I slowly lower the dumbwaiter down the black shaft to the O'Rourke's apartment, open the door a crack and listen. I have all my clothes on in case the dumbwaiter cord snaps and I crash into the basement. I don't want the super to find my broken body in underwear. Nor my mother or father.

The O'Rourke's apartment is an exact duplicate of ours. I scramble into their kitchen, creep past Joan's parents' bedroom. They're both snoring. Before I turn the corner to the next hallway I hear her brother taking a leak. The bathroom light is on. When he goes back to his room I crawl toward Joan's room. Her door is open. Her six-year old sister is in the bed too. Joan motions to me to get under the covers. She's wearing flannel pajamas. We don't say anything. We don't do anything, either. We just hold on to each other. If her sister wakes up I know she'll scream "HELP, SÉAMUS IS IN MY BED." Mr O'Rourke will kill me right here. He has nothing to lose since he's going to prison anyhow.

We doze for a while.

"I'll miss you."

"I'll miss you too," she says. "I hope you'll write to me."

"Of course I will." I kiss her. "Good night Joan."

I creep down the hall into the kitchen and climb into the dumbwaiter. I pull hard on the rope and reach the fourth floor.

The Donovans in 4A must have left a cake or pie on their kitchen table. All the roaches in the dumbwaiter shaft are lined up taking turns slipping through a small crack into their kitchen. No roaches in 5A tonight.

Dumbwaiter Romeo. Craziest thing I've ever done. I could have been caught. Gotten Joan into trouble. Could have been hurt. It's hard to explain. She needed me.

HE'S DONE IT again, mom," my sister Siobhan shrieks.

"Are you sure darling?" my mother asks. "He's such a lovely boy. Why would he do something so terrible?"

"I just came up the stairs and didn't see Marty anywhere," I say.

"I didn't see anyone either," Siobhan says.

"He wouldn't expose himself to you Siobhan. You're only in the sixth grade. I'm in high school. And so is Marty."

"Now, don't use that horrible word *expose*," my mother scolds.

"Expose isn't the whole truth," Siobhan yells. "He has all his clothes off and everything he has is out there. He has a Safeway paper bag over his head."

"Lord help us," my mother says. "A bag over his head. He's really sick."

"You don't look at him, do you?" I chide.

"Séamus. Of course I don't look."

"Then how could you tell it's a bag from Safeway?"

"The bag is what I look at. And it isn't funny. I'm scared to death he'll attack me right there on the stairs." Siobhan starts to sob. "God knows what he might do to me."

Every day, students at St Nick's return to their apartments for lunch. For the past few days Siobhan swears Marty O'Toole in 4D has been taking off his clothes. When he hears her coming up the stairs he opens his apartment door and steps out on the landing.

"If I tell your father, he'll kill Marty," my mother says. "We have to come up with a plan to confront him."

My mother says she can run down to the fourth floor when Siobhan is coming up and catch him in the filthy act. Or I could hide behind Siobhan coming up the stairs then jump out and nail him.

Then I came up with a foolproof plan. I have a Univex Aim-And-Shoot Camera with a Synchro-Flash Unit, guaranteed to take needle sharp pictures.

"Snap." I say. "We'll have documented evidence he's showing himself to Siobhan. With a bag over his head, he won't see the camera."

I walk home from school with Siobhan. She starts up the stairs and I follow a few paces behind. My mother and Sinead are waiting on the fifth floor. I'm ready for the fourth floor photo shoot.

Siobhan screams: "I got you now, Marty. I've got proof you're a pig,"

He's just as Siobhan says. Stark naked. I snap his picture.

"You poor darling," my mother says.

"He didn't know what hit him," Siobhan says. "He didn't have anything on so he couldn't chase me up here. Oh, sweet revenge."

We eat our liverwurst sandwiches and gloat over our success.

"Oh no," I say sadly. "Photo processors will never print a picture of someone naked. If they find nudity in a roll of film they're required to destroy the negative and the print."

Our once happy family lunch group is dejected.

"Doesn't Danny's brother Chris do some developing?" Siobhan asks.

Chris agrees to develop the film. He confides he has never developed a nude before and what a shame it has to be a boy.

In his closet we watch the image appear on a white sheet of paper.

"Whew," Chris says. "Marty's endowed."

"I think he's in a state of excitement," I laugh.

He enlarges the photo to eight by ten and makes two copies.

"That's what I've seen every day this week," Siobhan says. "That's Marty with the Safeway bag."

"Oh, my sweet little girl," my mother says, taking Siobhan into her arms. "My poor precious little girl. What a horrible experience. He's a very sick boy."

I've never seen my mother fighting mad. "I'm taking this disgusting photo to 4D. To Mrs O'Toole."

When she returns, my mother is trembling. "I told Mrs O'Toole that Marty has been in the hall every day this week," my mother says. "She looked at the photo and said she could see the 4D on the door, but who's to say the person with the paper bag on his head is Marty. She said it could be you, Séamus."

"Sometimes I'm a prankster, but I'd never do anything like that," I say.

"I explained to her that you are blond, and that patch there's definitely black. Mrs O'Toole said she's seen me shopping in Safeway so the bag could also have come from our apartment. She said I had the wrong person, that's for sure. She took the photo and slammed the door in my face. The O'Tooles are *shanty Irish.*"

"What do we do now?" I ask. "Send the photo to *Life Magazine*?"

"We do nothing," my mother says. "We just wait and see."

While the O'Flynn children want resolution, patience is one of my mother's strongest virtues.

Marty never appeared in the hall again. Mrs O'Toole never said another word to my mother.

SIXTEEN

Ten cents I earn carrying Safeway groceries for old ladies in the O'Flynn baby carriage gets me into the Lowe's Paradise Movie Theater on the Grand Concourse. It's a ten-minute walk from the dreary lobby at 222 to the majestic lobby of the movie theater. Gold gilt, oriental carpets, antiques, statuary, garlands, vaulted ceiling and gallerias. The vast theater auditorium has flying cherubs, copies of Greek and Roman statuary, heavy draperies, strutting peacocks along balcony railings, statues of gold lions on top of towering walls, all presided over by a statue of Lorenzo de'Medici in a wall niche. The nuns, even though they have never been inside, tell us the style of the Paradise Theater is Italian Renaissance slightly overdone, some of it copied from the Baroque church near the Vatican, Rome's Santa Maria della Vittoria.

If the movie is boring I lie back in my seat and stare up at the black sky sparkling with hundreds of twinkling stars mysteriously veiled by puffy moving clouds. Brian Deeney, a high school senior and usher at the theater shows me the crawl space above the ceiling. I see hundreds of tiny electric lights that fabricate the firmament and projectors that beam vaporous moving clouds onto the ceiling. The massive walls aren't really marble; they're made from plaster and straw because it's an inexpensive way to build majestic structures. So what if it's a fantasy *paradise*. I know the movies aren't real either but I still look forward to Saturday afternoons.

Theater seats on the right are for children without parents. A matron in a nurse's uniform patrols the aisles with her flashlight. She's looking for perverts who sneak into the children's section. I don't think she's ever caught one. Creeps seem to seek out women who are alone in the theater. When the action on the screen is riveting and you're hanging onto every word, there's a piercing shriek and a woman is bashing a masher over the head with her pocketbook. The police haul the molester to jail. I spend most Saturday afternoons in the Paradise. Always two movies, a few cartoons and Movietone News. Lights never come on. Nonstop entertainment. If I like a movie, I'll stay to see it a second, or even a third time.

The saddest movie I ever saw was about a dying mother. I never thought about losing my mother or father. I thought you just upped and died and then had a funeral mass at St Nick's. The boy in the movie is learning death can take weeks, months or years. I'm certain there'll be a happy ending. But she dies. When the movie ends I don't get out of my seat. I don't even want to be cheered up by the eternally twinkling stars and moving indoor clouds. My eyes are brimming. I'm embarrassed. Danny asks me what's the matter. Nothing much. Maybe, too many Tootsie Rolls.

MR SCHMIDT WAS standing on the edge of the roof. Mrs McGinty across the street saw him and called the police. She called my mother and said don't go out in the street. Call everyone in your building. Warn them. Mr Schmidt in 218 Loring may jump. He could land on you.

When we walk up Loring Place an ambulance is pulling out from 222. Our mothers are on the sidewalk.

"Don't look Siobhan," my mother says.

"Don't look at what?"

"Over there by the stoop."

"Looks like left over cold spaghetti," Danny says.

"It's hideous. Close your eyes," Danny's mother says.

"Do you remember the woman who recently jumped off the Empire State Building?" Mrs McGinty asks. "She landed on a parked diplomatic limousine. The car looked like it had been bombed by a German Luftwaffe. Can you imagine if she had landed on someone just taking a stroll along Thirty-Third Street?"

"Mrs McGinty, you shouldn't be talking about that right now," my mother says. "The children are home for lunch."

My sisters run upstairs.

Mr Schmidt landed on the sidewalk between our stoop and the lone maple tree.

Mr Shaughnessy, the new 222 superintendent, argues with Mr Zuck, super of 218. "Schmidt lived in your building," Shaughnessy says to Zuck. "You hose it down. It's your responsibility."

Zuck says: "The bloody hair and skin bits are in front of 222, not 218. It's not my problem."

"This is disgusting," says Mrs Daly. "Give me the hose." She adjusts the nozzle to the strongest stream and aims it at the mess on the sidewalk.

"Séamus, let's go upstairs."

My mother says it was a good thing Mr Schmidt, *Lord have mercy on him*, didn't jump just as we were coming up the hill.

"What would you like for lunch?" my mother asks.

"Nothing," Siobhan says.

"Nothing," Sinead says.

"I'm not hungry," I say.

My mother is crying.

THE RAFFERTY BROTHERS' Funeral Parlor is across the street from St Nick's on University Avenue. In Ireland bodies are waked at home. There's sadness of course, but the strong belief in an afterlife helps turn the gloom into a celebration with food and drinks.

Since my father has two jobs he's never available to accompany my mother to Rafferty's wakes. My mother insists I be the male mourner. Horror movies have already turned me into a full-fledged coward. The number one terrifying scene is in Dracula. Two thieves go to the cemetery to steal jewelry left on a corpse. They enter a mausoleum and spot a casket. They pry open the lid and move closer. Too close. Dracula is just waking up. He grabs an arm. I can feel the unearthly strength of Dracula's hand as he drags the robber slowly into the coffin. Once he's inside with Dracula the lid creaks closed. I can still hear the screams. And the panicked breathing and squeals of the lucky thief who gets away.

When my mother asks me to go with her to Raffertys I tell her I don't think I'm a good candidate for wake-hopping. My mother doesn't like me to make fun of the dead. "Séamus, I'm not hopping around the city going to wakes. These are relatives and friends of ours. I'm just following the commandment to bury the dead. The faithful departed need prayers. The poor souls in purgatory are stuck until enough prayers are said down here to get them into heaven."

"My he's growing so tall, Kit," Mrs Lenahan says to my mother. I'm the only boy in the funeral parlor. My mother drags me to *the last respects line*. Mr Finn, who lived up the street, was only forty-one when he died changing a light bulb. He was standing on a kitchen chair when his wife saw him crash to the floor. Mrs Finn thought he had put his finger in the socket and was electrocuted. "Heart, just stopped beating," my mother says. "The Lord said you'll never know the day or the hour. For Mr Finn it was February 26 at seven-ten p.m."

"I don't want to get too close," I say. "I can see him from here."

"It's an old Irish tradition to hold the deceased's hand," my mother says.

"Not me."

"Séamus, kneel down on this *prie-dieu* with me."

She takes hold of Mr Finn's hand and squeezes it, mumbling some prayers.

"Touch him Séamus."

"No."

"You don't have to hold his hand if you don't want to. Just touch it."

"No."

I have my hands clasped in prayer. She takes my finger and slowly rubs it along Mr Finn's hand.

"I'm going to throw up and that will cause as much commotion as the hunchback sitting up in his coffin."

"See. That isn't so bad. Good basic training for real life," my mother says. I hurry to the bathroom to wash my finger. I turn the wrong way. I'm in a room used to prepare bodies. That must be Mr Rafferty under the mask. He's dressed in doctor's scrub clothes. He turns to me with dried blood and wet blood all over rubber gloves. A pump is droning. It smells like a gas station.

"Yeesss?"

"Nnnooo," I say. I run out to the hall and into another waking room. I'm alone with another corpse in a casket surrounded by flowers.

I'm living inside a nightmare at Raffertys.

"Séamus, you're flushed," my mother says. "Bronchitis coming on again?"

IN A RECURRING dream I find a stash of coins in a white cloth pouch. I open the drawstring and pour the coins on the kitchen table. I fill both hands and then let the coins fall through my fingers dancing and jingling as they bounce on the Formica. I hear steam heat banging and clanking its way from the basement furnace to my bedroom. A soothing hiss of steam escapes the radiator valve. I'm holding a horde of half dollars, quarters, dimes and nickels. I grip them harder. I think of things I can buy. I'm eating a Woolworth's Chocolate and Vanilla Banana Royal. It tastes better in my dream than a real banana split. I get a surprising thrill taking one, two, three nickels from the pouch to pay for the Banana Royal. *Hiiiiissssss.* Warmth radiates my bedroom. I'm coming out of my dream. I squeeze my hands tighter. I slowly open my eyes and look over the covers at my tightly gripped hands. I'm holding the coins so tight my fingers hurt. I'm thrilled I can take the coins from this far off place and transport them into my bedroom. I know the money isn't mine, but this adds to the thrill. Finally, I open my cupped hands expecting a shower of silver on my bed. Nothing.

Why does spending money that is not mine give me such pleasure in my dreams? Would I experience the same excitement if I paid the Woolworth's soda jerk with money I stole? I decide to find out if my feelings in the recurring dream are even close to being real. I'll steal some money, just a dollar or two. I could buy a lot of Banana Royals with two dollars. I could fill every seat at Woolworth's Soda Fountain on Fordham Road and pick up the whole tab. But who can I steal from? My mother only has a few dollars in her purse. I know I'd feel rotten taking a dollar. My father's not a potential victim for this crime because he never carries money. He rides free to work on the railroad and brings a ham sandwich and Thermos of tea. I can't think of anyone else.

"Do you want to help me steal some money, Danny?" I ask. "I want the experience, just once. You can be my accomplice. You've helped me *liberate Esquire* magazines. Not too exciting. Let's pick someone's pocket."

"No way, Séamus. Count me out."

"I want to steal a few dollars, but don't have any prospects. Got any ideas?"

"I'm already sort of a pickpocket," Danny says. "My older brother hangs out at Mannion's Bar. In the morning when he's still knocked out from beer the night before, I rifle his pockets. He never misses the change I take."

"That's not exciting."

"If you saw my brother in a rage, you'd realize the chance I'm taking."

Since we can't come up with someone to steal from, we decide to steal *something*. Like from Safeway. I know Danny likes peanuts and eats a whole bag every time we go to Yankee Stadium. Let's steal a can of Planter's Peanuts.

"Well," Danny says, "If I'm going to be an accomplice, let's go for the big can."

The Safeway manager, Mike, asks us why we don't have our baby carriages with us on such a busy Saturday morning. We made enough last Saturday for today's movie. Besides we're playing football this morning.

"You boys are wonderful," Mike says. "You work hard to get what you want. When you get out of high school look me up. I'll get you a job at Safeway."

Danny thanks him for the compliment. He whispers to me maybe we should get out of here. I toss the football to Danny. I tell him to throw a pass to me. I let the ball bounce up the aisle. I pull off my football helmet and stuff it with a giant-size can of Planters.

"No backing out now," I say to Danny holding the helmet to my chest. We wrestle down the aisle and out the front door.

"See you next Saturday," Mike says.

My heart is pumping so fast it may break through my shirt. Danny looks over his shoulder to see if Mike is in pursuit. We run up Loring Place. Yes, the excitement I'm feeling exceeds the sensation I get in my dream where I always end up clutching only air. Today there's a payoff, a helmet full of peanuts. On the roof we open the can.

"Yuummm," Danny says, "Roasted peanuts, no shell to crack. Great idea, Séamus."

"I like peanut butter better," I say. "Peanut butter and grape jam on Wonder Bread."

We eat half the can. Now what do we do with the rest?

"Want to put them under your bed, Séamus?"

"No my mother will find them and ask too many questions."

Now I'm concerned. Mike may notice the can is missing. Word could be out all over the neighborhood. Mike will remember we didn't carry groceries today. We're prime suspects.

"We should've taken the smaller can," Danny says. "How are we going to get rid of the evidence?"

"My fingerprints are all over the can." I say.

"For one can of missing peanuts I don't think Safeway is going to call in Dick Tracy," Danny says.

"I wonder if they'll dock Mike's pay check to make up for the peanuts?"

"It's too late to put the peanuts back, Séamus."

In the basement Danny opens the furnace door. I toss the can far back on the burning coals.

"We're giving the nuts a double roasting," Danny chuckles. "Maybe the odor of roasted peanuts will hiss out of all the radiators upstairs."

I don't laugh.

When my coin-clutching dream ends I feel let down for a few moments. At the Paradise Theater that afternoon I didn't even enjoy *Gulliver's Travels*. Maybe my father's right about larceny. *Liberating* something seems to make more sense than stealing.

I'M ALWAYS IN a hurry. I don't want to wait. I want everything now. Sure my mother preaches about my selfishness. There are others you have to consider. Slow down. Take your time. My mother may not have a lot of education but she believes common sense often produces more results than book learning. When I get testy my mother sits me down and offers some common sense...

Patience is a virtue
Possess it if you can
It's always in a woman
Rarely in a man

"Your father doesn't have patience either. He comes in here from work, asks me to scrub his back and have dinner ready at the same time. Then he rushes out the door to his job at the Yacht Club. Notice how patient your sisters are. They don't complain about losing time when I tie their hair in rags. They help do the dishes and vacuum the apartment with charm and grace. Now Séamus you're the opposite. You're demanding. You want every wish fulfilled at the exact moment the idea comes into your head. I see you from the window racing up and down Loring Place. You run home for your lunch and run back to school. You run down the stairs and run up the stairs. You jump out of bed in the morning and jump into bed at night. You've helped me paint the apartment. My paintbrush caresses the walls. Yours just about tears the plaster off. The only thing you do slowly is eating. I think it's because you don't like the food I cook. Only one male ever had patience. Job. The bible describes him as long-suffering, never giving into the devil. I have the patience of Job, especially where you're concerned, Séamus."

It's true, my mother does have bountiful patience. Maybe I don't have much because the old proverb says rarely in a man and I'm only a young man. That must be it. Patience will come later.

ON THE WAY to mass on Sunday I spot the green edge sticking out under a garbage can. I pass by and then go back. It could be a dollar bill.

My sister Siobhan says we'll be late so hurry up.

I investigate. I tug at the corner and it's a bill, a ten-dollar bill.

"What did you pick up, Séamus?" Siobhan asks.

"Nothing."

"Well you went after something. You put it in your pocket."

"Oh. It's just an old baseball card. Nothing important."

During mass I feel it in my pocket. When I have my head down at communion I take a good look. No mistake. A ten-dollar bill. I won't have to take my baby carriage to Safeway to earn my Saturday spending money. Let's see. I have enough to go to the movies once a week for two years. I can buy the second hand bicycle advertised for sale in the hardware store. They're asking twelve dollars. Learning from my mother's bargaining skills I can probably negotiate the price down to ten. When they see me pull a big bill out of my pocket they'll know I mean business. I may even find a Kodak Vigilant Six camera in a pawnshop. This is the most exciting thing that's ever happened to me.

I hide the bill in my drawer, way at the bottom, under my *Esquires.* I almost forget to say my prayers. That's how the biggest dilemma I ever faced came to a head. As I start my prayers I think someone in the parish is probably crying right now. They lost ten dollars, a staggering amount of money. I reach down and pull out the bill. I sniff it. Perhaps I can tell who lost it. Slight perfume odor. Must be a woman. Oh no. It's a woman on the way to St Nick's. On the way to the eight o'clock mass. Her husband is probably yelling at her now. What do you mean you lost ten dollars? That would have fed our family for weeks. I hope he doesn't smack her. I hope he's not like Mr McCarthy. I push the bill back to the bottom of the draw. The prospects of what I can do with so much money gets me thinking again. A used Lionel electric train set. I've always wanted an electric train but only have the windup model.

I bring the bill to school. I'm not listening to Sister Helen teaching us religion. I know what I have to do.

After school I ring the rectory bell. Father Kelly says come in Séamus. How can I help you? I tell him about the ten-dollar bill. He says he will put a notice in the church bulletin, not mentioning the amount. I give him the bill for safekeeping.

I see the announcement the next Sunday. I'm hoping no one else sees it. But Father Kelly goes further. At the end of his sermon he mentions money was found last Sunday near Goldstein's Candy Store on Fordham Road. Contact the rectory if you want to make a claim.

At two p.m. he calls me and says come to the rectory.

Mrs Lenahan, who lives in the white six-story elevator building on Loring Place, is smiling. So is Father Kelly. Mrs Lenahan gives me the biggest tips on my Saturday grocery deliveries.

"Séamus, I lost the ten dollars," Mrs Lenahan says. "I was paying for the paper on the way home from mass. It must have fallen out of my wallet."

There go all my dreams. Well only half my dreams. Mrs Lenahan gives me a reward of five dollars.

SEVENTEEN

Before I played on the Loring Lions Baseball Team I had to go through the *Rite of Passage.* It's spring now and time for our new outfielder, Steve Houlihan and first baseman Paul Shea, to go through the ceremony.

Danny brings a large jar half full of lemonade. Ray pops out his *shillelagh* and takes a short leak into the jar. We do the same, joking about the various shades of yellow holy waters streaming from seven altar boys. Even doctored up it still looks like lemonade.

Steve and Paul are here now for their first practice at the Reservoir diamond.

"You're about to join the fearsome Lions," Danny says. "A winning team is formed when all players bond." Danny tries to sound serious. "Don't worry. We're not going to cut your wrist to intermingle our blood. Instead we've prepared a punch of magical juices which will help us to be the best street baseball team in St Nick's parish. This nectar will transform Steve into one of the world's greatest outfielders, Joe DiMaggio, and Paul into the revered first baseman, Lou Gehrig."

"Who gave you the recipe? Charles Atlas?" Steve asks.

"Only Loring Lions know. We wouldn't want the Andrews Avenue or Sedgwick Avenue teams to learn about our secret elixir."

Steve complains the juice is warm and tastes like very sour lemons. Paul says it tastes great. We know he's lying.

"You've been baptized with the sacred waters of the Lions. You have drunk from the streams of life."

"Why are you all laughing?" Paul asks.

"We'll tell you after the game. Here comes Andrews Avenue. Let's play ball."

No one has ever gotten sick after the Baseball Rite. But during the game I notice Steve bending over, obviously in pain.

On the way home we tell Paul and Steve about the *urine-ade.* They're good-natured and say we can't wait till next year's *Rite of Passage.* Paul says he won't take a piss for a whole day so his donation will really be rotten.

I ask Steve if he's O.K. as we walk up the stairs of 222. He lives on my floor in 5D. "It's not the Lions' lemonade," Steve says. "I've had sharp pains in my stomach for a week."

"Take care of yourself. We need you," I say. "We beat Andrews Avenue because you caught those two deep fly balls."

An ambulance took Steve to the hospital. His appendix had burst, probably while he played his first baseball game with the Lions.

Sister Helen Marie tells us Father Kruger is coming to our classroom.

"You know the whole school has been praying for one of your classmates, Steve Houlihan," Father Kruger says. "Poison from his appendix severely infected his other organs. The doctors did all they could. I gave him the last rites. I'm very sorry to tell you Steve died an hour ago. His passing was very peaceful. His whole family was at his side. Many of you have known Steve since he came to St Nick's in the first grade. He was a beautiful young man in every way. Sometimes it's difficult to understand why the Lord decided to call Steve at such a tender age to be with him now in Heaven."

Some girls in the class are crying. Sister Helen pulls a handkerchief from her habit and dabs the corner of her eyes. I stare at Steve's empty desk across the room. We often had competitive races up the stairs at 222. He won a few of our dashes to the top of the Empire State. He was soon to graduate. His death didn't make sense. The Houlihans needed Steve more than God did.

Father Kruger says the Houlihans can clothe Steve in his altar boy's black cassock and white surplice. He was waked for two days in the living room of 5D. I've never seen so many people sobbing before or since. I went across the hall and visited Steve a few times. I held on to his hand. That he was cold didn't matter at all. Mrs Houlihan put her arm around me and thanked me for coming. "I'm sorry for your trouble," I say. That's what I hear my mother say. Now I know the meaning of trouble. It hurts and hurts and hurts.

I'm in the boys' choir at the funeral mass. Father Kruger and all the parish priests are on the altar. Steve's coffin is sprinkled with holy water. Clouds of smoke from burning incense cover the casket.

"Steve's an angel in heaven," my mother says. "He's catching a ball in the outfield right now."

My imagination refused to stretch that far.

"WHAT'S THE MATTER Séamus?" my mother asks.

"Ooohhhhh. Nothing. Ooouuuccchhhh."

"For nothing, you're making a lot of racket. Is it a toothache?

"No."

"Yes it is. Your face is swollen. Why are you hiding your pain?"

"For good reason. I'm not going to that guy across the street."

"Well, sleep on it then."

I dreaded going to bed with a chunk of cotton soaked in oil of cloves seeping into my cavity. This is the worst ache I've ever had. I'll have to go to that crazy dentist tomorrow.

"I'm dying mom. Call Dr. Archibald."

"You're not going to that madman are you?" Sinead asks. "He's a drunk. He doesn't give Novocain. You're going to pass out from the pain."

"I'm going to die now from the pain. Why can't I go to some other dentist, who gives gas or at least enough Novocain so I don't feel anything?"

"Séamus, Dr. Archibald is here on Loring Place and half the price of fancy dentists on Fordham Road."

"That's the point," Sinead says. "He's cheap because he only gives you a few drops of Novocain. And he has the shakes."

"We can't afford a Fordham Road dentist, with big overhead."

"Ah ha. You admit he isn't a good dentist."

"He's good enough for the O'Flynns. I'm calling him now."

The throbbing increases. I try to keep my breath away from the cavity. "He can take you right now. I told him it's an emergency and you can stay home from school."

"See mom, he can take Séamus right away because no one can take the pain he gives out. St Rita's stigmata is nothing compared to his bloodletting."

"Stop upsetting Séamus. He'll do fine. I'll start praying for you in about fifteen minutes."

"Start now, *pleeeasee.*"

Dr. Archibald is in a basement apartment. I ring his bell and he opens the door immediately like he's stationed there waiting for someone, anyone.

"Good morning, Séamus," he smiles through crooked stained teeth. He's the one who should be going to the dentist.

I mumble something about the morning not being so good. He is trembling. His white coat makes his face look even grayer. He has a few tufts of brown-gray hair above each ear, a glistening baldhead and an oversized handlebar moustache.

"Let me have a look, Séamus. That's a whopping big cavity you've got in there. Last molar on the right. It must be painful. We'll just yank it, I mean pull it, out. It's a tooth you don't need."

Doctor Archibald's nose is almost inside my wide-open mouth.

"First we'll give you a little Novocain."

That's the problem. *Too little.*

"This is an oversized tooth Séamus. One root is going this way, the other that way. I can't pull it straight up and out. I'm going to saw the tooth in half then extract one piece this way, the other that way."

If I run out of here, I'll still have this excruciating pain. My tongue and lip start to tingle. Maybe it's a new type of Novocain, small dose, powerful result.

I close my eyes tight. I don't want to see instruments. Splitting the tooth is first. He's using a small buzz saw. I can smell the smoke coming out of my mouth. I can taste burning enamel, or is it the collapsing cavity?

"There. The cavity was so deep, your tooth cracked easily." His hands look like Mr Rafferty's, the undertaker. But this is my blood.

"Now a tug this way, and look Séamus, the first root is out. Well almost out."

"One down, one root to go." He sounds exhausted.

"Another tug that way." I still don't open my eyes but I think he's put his foot on the edge of the chair to give himself more leverage. "I've got it. No more pain for Séamus."

Dr. Archibald leaves me in the chair pressing down a wad of gauze on the wound. In the kitchen around the corner I hear a bottle clink against a glass. I guess his pain never goes away.

EIGHTEEN

Headlines in New York newspapers tell you today how hot you were yesterday.

NEW YORK SIZZLES.

SCORCHER.

HEAT WAVE.

My father says black tar on apartment roofs soak up the sun. And 5A is on the top floor, inches under the blistering tar. My mother puts pitchers of ice water in every bedroom. Windows are wide open. Fans drone out of every window in the alleyway. I stretch out on my bed in shorts. No movement. If I move I sweat.

The coolest spots in the neighborhood are the basement church at St Nick's or the Harlem River. Parents warn us about the dank Harlem full of strange filthy things floating by.

Orchard Beach, operated by the New York City Parks Department, is a favorite place to cool off. It's in the eastern Bronx on Long Island Sound. We call it *Horseshit Beach.* It's usually polluted and signs say CLOSED FOR SWIMMING. What are you supposed to do on a scalding beach? Sit there and think how cool it would be if sewage hadn't washed down from Westchester and Connecticut homes. Besides I need bus fare to get there.

Another popular swimming hole is in the Bronx Zoo, a milky pond the color of a pale green egg-cream surrounding Monkey Island. Monkeys don't like the heat either. They get testy and nip you if you get too close to their island. Parkees patrol the wooded shore area because naked bathers use the pond when the Bronx is scorching. They wait till you come back to your clothes and tell you adamantly no swimming allowed at the zoo. The few girls claiming their clothes seem to get much better treatment from the parkees.

The Harlem River is only a few blocks from Loring Place. No bus fare. No one bothers you. No cops around, just railroad workers. Drop your clothes. Dive off rocks into the fast moving cocoa-brown current.

The Harlem is an arm of the Hudson River. At the northern tip of Manhattan Island most of the flow from the Hudson continues along the west side of the island and the eastern shores of New Jersey. But some of the Hudson's waters flow left to form the mouth of the Harlem River. The two rivers converge into violent whirlpools at Spuyten Duyvil. Dutch settlers in the early seventeenth century were determined to navigate these whirling eddies "in spite of the devil."

"Let's swim over to the Manhattan shore," Ray challenges. The Harlem is about a half mile wide at Spuyten Duyvil. You have to be a strong swimmer to end up directly across from where you dive in. If you tire, you'll be swept bareassed down the river far from your clothes. Another favorite swimming spot on the Harlem is at the northern end of Manhattan Island, just below Columbia University football field. A crevasse in the rocks creates diving perches from a few feet above the river to the height of a five-story apartment. After a few dives we stretch out on the rocks in the sun. Now we're ready to swim back to the Bronx shore.

I opened my eyes underwater only once. Under the Harlem is dark brown nothingness with a trace of muddy yellow light at the surface. Floating by are scumbags and turds. Condoms create a mystery for us. We know what they are used for. Fish them out with a stick and stretch them on a rock. Don't get too close. Never touch it. Don't breathe. Snaring one with a knot wins the competition. Locked in is the whole wad. Are those tadpoles still alive? The cold water probably refrigerates them. How do hundreds of condoms get into the river each night? At first we think they're flushed down the toilets of thousands of apartments lining the river in the Bronx and Manhattan. Ray Fitzgerald's brother, who works for the city, kills this theory. None of the sewage entering the river comes from apartment buildings. The huge sewers along the Harlem River are used only for rainwater drainage.

Then we think it must be the passengers riding in the all-private bedroom silver bullet train, the *20th Century Limited.* The Limited leaves Grand Central Station every night for Chicago racing along express tracks under Manhattan, coming above ground along the Harlem River. I know all train toilets flush onto the tracks. I think railroad workers find the scumbags the next day and toss them into the river. I ask my father what time the Limited leaves at night. When he tells me six p.m., I figure the train streaks past Spuyten Duyvil forty-five minutes later. This causes another dilemma for our gang. Could you possibly do the whole thing in less than an hour and flush the evidence from the rocketing train by 6:45? Aren't most passengers men going to Chicago on business? What about Catholics on the train? They can't use condoms. Then why are there so many every day?

One Sunday we notice the number of condoms increases. We're certain now it's because of the hundreds of boaters on the Hudson on Saturday from Tarrytown, Hastings, Dobbs Ferry, Irvington and Nyack. "They're pleasure boaters who have some extra pleasure on the Hudson," Ray laughs.

THE CIRCLE CRUISE dayliner is coming up the Harlem. It's a muggy ninety-nine degrees.

"Here come the tourists from Illinois and Iowa," says Danny. "Let's show them our stuff."

We let out a shrieking Tarzan cry as the dayliner comes close. A roar begins as the first sightseers spy naked kids standing on the rocks. Tourists on the right side of the boat rush to the left side. Binoculars focus and cameras click. The dayliner tilts deep into the water on the left side. The captain barks his order to move back to the other side so the boat will straighten up. No one obeys.

Larry Nolan starts the entertainment diving off the rock closest to the river. I'm about half way up and I go next, followed by Danny higher up. Ray Fitzgerald has the most guts and his finale is a perfect swan dive into the murky Harlem. Tourists roar approval. Cheers and whistles.

MY CLAIRVOYANT COUSIN Mavourneen Collins drops by for tea. She has mystical powers and can predict the future. At least that's what my mother believes.

Mavourneen is a greenhorn and looks like a gypsy. She's as white as Ivory soap, with blazing red hair. Her chin comes to a point and there are unmatched free-forms of rouge on each cheek. I stare at her intently as she sips the last few drops of tea.

My mother whispers so the spell isn't broken: "Séamus wonders if you could tell him how he's going to fare in high school?"

Mavourneen stares into her cup. She turns it so my mother and I can see the clumps of black tea leaves on the bottom and running up one side.

"Huummm," she says stroking the ostrich feather poking out of her diminutive red felt hat.

Her dangling earrings dance from side to side. Her eyes roll. She smiles. Her eyes roll. She frowns.

"Do you see these two parallel lines snaking along the bottom of the cup?" It's a river. The River Shannon. Or is it the Liffey? It's getting clearer now. I see, it's the Harlem River."

"Oh, my God," my mother cries. "Séamus swims there every day in the summer."

"Susshhh," Mavourneen says. "Look. See the horns. Oh my lord, big horns. It's the devil himself. He's on the rocks. I see large boulders. They're running up the side of my cup. I see Séamus. He's getting ready to dive into the river. Now he's in the air......." Mavourneen stops. She keeps her head down.

"Go on. Please go on," my mother pleads.

"Not with Séamus here. I can't."

"Séamus is a young man now. He's going to graduate in a few months. He can take it. Can't you Séamus?"

"Please Cousin Mavourneen. Tell me what's going to happen in high school."

"Séamus, don't break the spell," my mother pleads. "Mavourneen, please tell us what the leaves are saying."

"You're in the air now, Séamus. The devil is watching you. You haven't pushed out far enough. The rock at the water's edge. Your head is.... *Ohhhhhh...*"

"Mavourneen," my mother screams. "What is it? We must know. If we know the future we can change it. Séamus can stop swimming in the river right now. Can't you Séamus?

"Mom. Stop being hysterical. You told me Mavourneen's not always right. Let's start over. Make her another cup of tea."

"Séamus, I'm receiving a telepathic message," Mavourneen says. "Two O'Flynn lads in Ireland died at age THIRTEEN. Both drowned. Most Irishmen can't swim. Both were named Séamus."

"Jesus, Mary and Joseph. Protect us. Séamus is thirteen. We must change his name. His confirmation name is Patrick. We'll start calling him Paddy Junior."

"I'm sorry to bring such woeful tidings," Mavourneen says.

"Séamus. The devil Mavourneen sees in her teacup is the Spuyten Duyvil devil, the place where you swim in the river. Promise me you'll stop swimming there," my mother cries. "Go to Monkey Island. Go to Orchard Beach. Go where there are no rocks. The devil is around that part of the Harlem River."

The fog around Mavourneen lifts and her sunny disposition breaks through.

I rang Danny's bell. "I hope you want to go for a swim, Séamus," Danny says.

"That's exactly what I want to do. I've been scared to dive off the highest rock at Spuyten Duyvil. Today in spite of that damned devil, I'm going to swan into the air."

NINETEEN

I always know when it's cold enough for the ice hockey season to begin. When New York freezes, my eyes strangely spout warm tears.

In winter, the parkee who yells at us all summer, declares a truce. He floods the children's wading pool creating an ice rink at DeVoe Park, across from St Nick's Church. It's early January and there's a light dusting of snow on the stiff grass. A heavy snowfall is forecast. KEEP OFF THE GRASS signs will soon be covered with snow. When it's this cold in New York, I imagine a light tap on my frozen ear will shatter it into a thousand pieces. Breath becomes glazed frost.

We choose up sides to play hockey with a flat river washed rock as the puck.

"Hello, Séamus," the man in a black overcoat says as I skate along the edge of the frozen pool. I can't see who called me. His face is hidden by the wide brim of a black fedora. There's no sign of a Roman collar, but I remember that voice. It's Father Cronin. I skate quickly to the other side of the ice.

I never told anyone what he did to me in front of my parents. I don't think anyone would believe me. Now I want to whack him in the face with my hockey stick.

When I coast past him I say, "Go back to Brooklyn, Father."

THE FIRST SNOWFALL is an excuse to skip homework and go to the park. It's a clear January night. The moon throws long charcoal fir and pine shadows across the snow.

Four sleds are lined up for the eighth grade race, boys on bottom, girls on top. Alice Mayhew belly flops on top of me. I didn't invite her. She chose my sled. She's just one of the girls who occasionally hang around. She's pretty enough, but I wish it had been Joan O'Rourke or Eileen Kelleher. Racing down hill almost out of control my sled seems to be drifting into slow motion. Alice is bouncing on and off me, our legs wrapped tightly. It's as if I'm high in a tree watching *this* girl and *that* boy having fun, rising and falling. I've never been this close to anyone, except Joan and she's way out in Montauk. Shrieks and laughter seem far away. Her cheek is close to me now. Her hair whips across my face.

"Séamus, Séamus," she says laughing.

"Hold tighter, Alice."

I've had strange stirrings the past few months. Ray and Danny keep making comments about taking sex into my own hands. Stories about saying goodbye to venial sins, and hello to mortal sins. Sins that send you to hell.

"Hey, look at Séamus," Ray chides. "Alice made him rise and shine." Danny whacks me on the back and clips my fly. Tommy hits me with a snowball. "You've been slow, Séamus. Welcome to our elite St Nick's group. Welcome to the Eighth Grade Mortal Sinners Club."

NOW THAT I'M an altar boy I've gotten to know the St Nick's priests better. But there's a downside. When I go to confession they recognize my voice.

On each confessional box there's a plaque naming the priest inside. You get to pick the priest who'll hear your confession. Since I joined the Mortal Sinners Club I only go to Father Gallagher. He's retired, has heart disease, wears bottle thick glasses and two hearing aids.

It's four p.m. Saturday afternoon. The priests are going into the confessionals. I get on the end of the longest line. We all know Father Gallagher is a pushover.

"Psssttt, Séamus. Come in here." It's Father Kelly sticking his head through dark maroon curtains. "Don't go to Father Gallagher. I'm just sitting here waiting for someone."

He knows me too well. How can I get out of here? I could have a sudden attack of bronchitis. I could snort, wheeze, whistle, cough and then go home.

"Séamus, come here." He's adamant.

I'm on my knees in the dark. Father Kelly pushes back the wooden slide. I only see his silhouette.

"Bless you Séamus. How long has it been since your last confession?"

"Two years. No, I mean two weeks."

"This is the first time you've come to me."

"I know." And it may be the last.

I know what I'm supposed to say to get things started. I should tell him how many times I did this and that. But I forget the sins I had listed carefully in my mind as I walked to St Nick's.

Father Kelly decides to help. "Have you used curse words, Séamus?"

"My father takes me to Holy Name Society meetings. They want to stop profanity. I'm careful. Maybe a *damn* now and then. But that's it."

He shouldn't be talking to me like we're old friends. He's not supposed to get personal.

"Anything else?"

"I threw a folding chair on the gym floor when we lost to the St Peter's team."

"Yes, and....."

I used to find confession easy. I knew how to examine my conscience. A few bad words uttered, some acts of disobedience, minor impure thoughts. Now there are some weighty issues I have to deal with every day, some every hour.

"I had impure thoughts."

"How many times?"

"*Lots*. I mean about a dozen since my last confession." I'm lying. It must be many dozen in the last two weeks. How can I remember ten of this, four of that? Should I keep a pad and pencil in my pocket and write down my sins? At the end of the day I could get weird enjoyment out of reading the list. That would be an additional sin. Being a good Catholic was easier before my *shillelagh* popped into my life.

"AND..." Long pause.

"I committed impure actions."

"Alone....or....with others?"

"Once with others and a few by myself."

"Who were you with?"

I can't believe this. He wants to know her name. I won't tell him. I don't have to tell him. That would be spreading scandal and that's another type of sin. I'm never going to get out of this box.

"Who were you with, Séamus?"

"A girl in my class."

"And what was the impurity?"

"I got excited when she jumped on top of me."

"Go on...."

"She jumped on top of my sled. I was already in a belly-flop position." Oh no. I shouldn't have said *position.*

"And...."

"Well, I got excited." I just hope Alice Mayhew isn't waiting on the other side of the confessional box. She could be listening to me spilling the beans.

"And...."

"She didn't know anything was going on. It wasn't her fault. My *shillelagh* is the problem. I didn't do a thing. He did. Well he really didn't do anything big. The race was over and that was the end of the evening."

"Séamus, you're not the first young man to come into puberty. You're beginning to experience temptations. That's normal. But you are a Soldier of Christ, and soldiers know how to defend themselves. They know how to fight. Besides you're Irish and they're the best fighters of all."

"Thank you, father."

"But you didn't finish your confession. You also said you committed impure actions by yourself. With hundreds of boys and girls in the parish you can imagine the number of abuse sins I hear about every Saturday afternoon."

The boys I know about. But did he say girls? That's impossible. They don't have the same equipment. But Danny and Ray say they have something that's very small and you can't see it unless you really search for it. Now I'm glad I came to Father Kelly. No sex education class at St Nick's. Only pick up a little here and there in the streets.

"Is there anything else you have to confess, Séamus?"

"I'm certainly going to try to cut *down*, I mean cut *out* impure actions. But when I fail again, and a car hits me crossing Fordham Road, am I really going to hell?"

"There's no doubt in my mind hell is real," Father Kelly says. "But it's important to understand no one's perfect. St Augustine, whose rule I follow as an Augustinian priest, was more than an ordinary sinner. In his book *Confessions* written in 397, that's fifteen hundred years ago, he said the madness of lust held him captive. He wrote about his muddy cravings of the flesh and the bubblings of first manhood. In his youth he said he was on fire. He lived with a young woman for many years and when he was eighteen she bore him a son."

St Augustine had an illegitimate baby? How did he become a saint?

Some of Father Kelly's sermon in the dark box is over my head. "Augustine confessed in his book about his illicit pleasures. He said he stank in the sight of God. St Augustine ultimately realized he was unhappy. He said every soul is unhappy when tied only to material things."

I'm surprised someone who's a saint had the same bubblings and cravings in 397.

"In your journey into manhood you are experiencing epiphanies, visions of good and evil, sudden illuminations, divine enlightenments. You'll do fine Séamus. For your penance say three Our Fathers and Three Hail Marys."

Father Kelly blesses me and closes the wooden slide. I've been in the confessional a long time. I open the drapes. Now there's a long line waiting. They probably think I had some incredible sins to confess.

Saints have always been up there somewhere. Untouchable. If St Augustine were around today we'd invite him to join our Mortal Sinners Club, probably as our Commander-In-Chief. I'd also tell him to go to Father Kelly for confession.

WE HAVE TO write a paper on the history of our family," Siobhan says.

"Mom you and dad need to tell me more about my grandparents and your brothers who were killed after immigrating to New York. I have to know everything about the O'Flynns and O'Learys. Sister Mary Ita says it doesn't all have to be good. She wants to know if there are any skeletons or horse thieves in our family."

"We didn't have horse thieves," my mother says, "but we had a respected horseman, my grandfather, Peter O'Leary. He was the first to be born in my family home in 1827. He inherited the fifty-acre farm and married Johanna O'Flynn, my grandmother. Years later, with the promise of life care in their home, they turned the farm over to my mother Marguerite and my father, William O'Leary. My grandmother who smoked a pipe every day, died at 86. When I came home from school my grandfather called *Kath-ah-leen, Kath-ah-leen* come up and light my pipe. He was blind and bedridden. He told me how much he missed my grandmother. He started to believe he was young again and wanted to drive his horse and buggy. We propped up my grandfather in his bed, put a chair in front of him and gave him a small whip. My brother Bill said *giddyup, giddyup* and my grandfather whipped the chair and bounced the bed. He was a wonderful man. He prayed God would take him. Six months to the day his wife died, he passed away. They were a real love match."

"That's horrible," my sister says. "I had a great-grandmother who smoked a pipe. I won't put that in my paper because I may have to read it in front of the class."

My father told my sister he traveled steerage on the ship taking him to New York. "My bed was in the lumpy black coal bin."

"Well, I am certainly not going to put that in my paper," Siobhan snapped. "Steerage is for *shanty Irish.*"

"That's more of your father's *malarkey*," my mother says. "Paddy, tell them the latest O'Flynn news."

"The O'Flynns have three girls and you, Séamus," my father says. "Next March we'll be having another boy."

"Now, how in God's name would ye be knowin' that?" my mother laughs.

"Cousin Mavourneen had tea at our apartment the other day. She saw our new little Mickey on the bottom of her cup."

TWENTY

All my life I've known only one President of the United States, Franklin Delano Roosevelt. He's coming to the Bronx.

President Roosevelt was elected in 1932, when I was a baby. My father listens to his fireside chats on the radio and I've seen our president at Saturday matinees in *Fox Movietone News* reels and in the *New York Daily News.* Roosevelt is Commander-In-Chief of our armed forces who are starting to win World War II in Germany and the South Pacific. Now he's coming to the Bronx. No one has ever been President four times, but Roosevelt warns it wouldn't be a good idea to *"change horses in midstream."* Republicans nominated Thomas Dewey who is governor of New York. Naturally, the Republicans want to stop Roosevelt. They spread rumors he's ill and won't be able to serve. But what really upset me, the Republicans made up a story about Fala, the President's dog.

President Roosevelt delivered a speech to Daniel O'Regan's Teamsters Union that contained a paragraph that may have turned the tide for Roosevelt:

The Republican leaders have not been content with attacks on me, on my wife, or on my sons...they now include my little dog, Fala. Well, of course, I don't resent them, and my family doesn't resent attacks, but Fala does resent them...You know Fala is Scotch...as soon as he learned that the Republican fiction writers had concocted a story that I had left him behind on the Aleutian Islands and had sent a destroyer back to find him--at a cost to the taxpayer of two or three or eight million dollars-his Scotch soul was furious. He has not been the same dog since.

To show he's in good health, Roosevelt plans a trip through New York City. Bronx Borough President James J. Lyons, a parishioner of St Nicholas, has been invited to ride in the President's open car as he tours the Bronx. He's also been asked by the White House to arrange an inspirational ceremony when the President comes by St Nicholas Church.

Father Kruger sends a letter home with all school children to come out for the big day, Saturday August 21st, 1944:

We at St Nicholas owe a great debt to our beloved President Roosevelt. He has dedicated his life to the common man, to the forgotten man, average Americans like us.

Before Roosevelt became president, he had nominated New York Governor Alfred E. Smith for President at the 1924 Democratic national convention. This was a bold and courageous act because his advisers told him it would be a major mistake to nominate a Roman Catholic for the President of the United States. This same resoluteness helped him overcome his physical disabilities from polio.

The thirty-fourth Psalm teaches us: "I sought the Lord, and he answered me; he delivered me from all my fears."

In his Inaugural address in 1933, President Roosevelt asked us to be optimistic about the future of America when he said "the only thing we have to fear is fear itself." Like the Lord, President Roosevelt has delivered us from our fears. Besides, he primed the economic pump, spending millions to create jobs and establish social programs benefiting all of us at St Nick's.

He has taken us from the depths of the Great Depression,through World War II, to what will surely soon be victory in Europe and the Pacific. Now we have a once in a lifetime opportunity to come out en masse to let the President know how all of us at St Nicholas Parish appreciate his labors on our behalf.

My father reveres F.D.R. and says the President is the reason the O'Flynns have such a comfortable, wonderful life in this country. My father and mother are pleased we begin each day at St Nick's School with a Pledge of Allegiance to the United States, followed by the Our Father.

"President Roosevelt seems tired," my father says. "He probably shouldn't run for a fourth term. Now those friggen

Republicans are spreading vicious rumors about Roosevelt. To prove they're wrong he's going to tour New York boroughs in an open car. The O'Flynns will be on the front steps of St Nick's to cheer him on to a fourth term." This is the only time I've seen my father on a soapbox.

"Besides," my mother adds, "the war is still raging in Europe and the Pacific. I agree with Roosevelt this would be a bad time to change horses. Our Republican Governor Dewey could get in. That would be a disaster for working men like your father."

"Are the Roosevelts bringing Fala?" Sinead asks.

"When they're in the touring car, Fala is always on the president's lap," I say enthusiastically. It seems the whole country loves the First Family's terrier.

After mass, Father Kruger tells my parents he's received a call from Borough President Lyons. "The Democratic National Committee wants St Nick's, one of the largest parishes in New York City, to do something special. His car will pass right here on our corner," says Father Kruger pointing to the intersection of Fordham Road and University Avenue.

"Now Father Kruger, do ye think there's a wee bit of politickin' goin' on?" my father thickens his brogue. "Could there be a hint of interest in the 12,000 votes we have here at little old St Nick's?"

"Forty-seven electoral votes are at stake in New York," Father Kruger says. "Some of those are right here in University Heights."

Father Kruger forms a President Roosevelt Welcoming Committee. He asks my father to be a member. The committee wants to do something BIG, something appropriate for such a large parish community. They decide to have a fifty-foot long American flag made. It will be rolled up and strung between the two church towers in front of the rose window.

Father Kruger tells the nuns he wants the entire Fife and Drum Corps from the parish's Sea Scouts on the church steps. Instead of my altar boy's cassock, I'll put on my sailor's uniform. We practice *"America The Beautiful."* Muriel Ann Camellia, who plays the xylophone on Sunday morning's "Horn & Hardart Automats Children's Hour," will direct the music.

"All school children are to dress in their white First Communion outfits, if they still fit," the note from Sister Catherine said.

Only one former president is still alive, Herbert Hoover. The only recollection I have of him from my history lessons is in 1931, the magical year of my birth, Boulder Dam, was renamed Hoover Dam in his honor. President Roosevelt took office in 1933. Two years later he changed the name back to Boulder Dam. "Politics," my father says. "In this case it was justified. During the Depression many Irish lived in the shanty *Hoovervilles* around the country. Besides, Hoover's a Republican."

The Presidential cavalcade started at nine-forty five in Brooklyn. Rain poured into the open car, but Roosevelt refused an umbrella. He wants the throngs to see him. The twenty-one-car caravan drives through the streets of Queens then over the Whitestone Bridge into the Bronx. Borough President Lyons is with the President. The roar of the crowds lining Fordham Road and University Avenue joins the clamor of thousands who hang out apartment windows or on fire escapes banging pots with big spoons or waving flags and placards.

"IT'S A DATE TILL '48 WITH ROOSEVELT"

"VICTORY WITH FRANKLIN D."

"HAIL OUR COMMANDER-IN-CHIEF"

Cheers, piercing whistles and "WE WANT ROOSEVELT" greet President and Mrs Roosevelt as the glistening black Packard touring car slows down in front of St Nick's. Roosevelt's wearing his favorite piece of clothing, his blue-black naval cape and felt fedora. Eleanor Roosevelt blends in with the sea of red, white and blue in a dark red fur collared coat. The Roosevelts are drenched.

"Welcome to the Bronx and St Nicholas Parish, Mr President," Father Kruger says into a microphone that broadcasts his voice through the Angelus bell system at the top of each tower of the church.

Sister Catherine presents a dozen American beauty roses to Mrs Roosevelt. Father Kelly pulls a cord loosening the enormous American flag. As it unfurls from the towers, Fala, startled, jumps onto the President's lap and barks at the flapping flag. Father Kruger leads the crowd in the Pledge of Allegiance.

I'm standing a few feet away from the man I have only seen in newsreels on Saturday mornings at the Paradise Theater. I blew extra breath into my fife....

"...God shed his light on thee
And crown thy good with brotherhood
from sea to shining sea...."

"Thank you St Nicholas, Cathedral of the Bronx. Thank you Borough President Lyons. Thank you Augustinian Fathers and Sisters of St Dominic," President Roosevelt says into the microphone, seated in his car. His voice is powerful. "This is what makes America great. Love of God and Country. Country and God. May God bless you and America."

TWENTY-ONE

Looking through lace curtains in the living room I see one of the towers of the George Washington Bridge, the one on the New York side. The bridge's steel is crisscrossed into an open weave so the winds over the Hudson River can pass through, like the warm summer breeze passing through my mother's fancy Irish lace curtains.

It's an hour's walk from Loring Place to the Washington Bridge. We walk or skate over the span to the New Jersey side and back again. I think about the female eels below who are now fat enough to swim down the Hudson. A few will end up on my father's fishing line. The others are swimming out to sea on the way to their Bermuda spawning grounds. I enjoy thinking about their life cycle but not the possibility of having eel again for dinner. The Circle Line Cruiser passes underneath. I see the Empire State Building a few miles downtown. When I'm in the Empire State I look north at the George Washington Bridge spanning the Hudson River.

Under the bridge is a large grassy area edging the Hudson. We come here to daydream. I lay back directly under the span that curves up toward the middle of the bridge, then slopes down till it reaches New Jersey at the Palisades Cliffs. The towers holding up the span are anchored into massive concrete embankments. I've heard a worker in 1931 fell into wet concrete and no one missed him till quitting time. The cement had hardened. I think of him entombed like the mummies I see in the Metropolitan Museum. Perhaps thousands of years from now an anthropologist will jackhammer the foundation and find him clutching his wrench.

The bridge span above me is part of Highway One that goes as far as the Pacific Ocean. My father doesn't know how to drive so I'll be the one to take my family to Los Angeles. I've picked the car I'm going to buy. A used 1939 Hudson Six Touring Sedan with Airfoam cushions, two-toned color with striking gleaming chrome that new costs $854. I also love the Hudson River, so why not have a car with the Hudson name. I'll probably have to wait ten years to get the money together to buy the used Touring Sedan. It's the only car with Auto-Poise Control that keeps wheels straight when a tire blows. My mom's a worrier; she'll like that safety feature. I'll only buy a used Hudson that also has the optional Weather-Master Fresh Air and Heat Control so I can use it on both coasts.

Passing under the Washington Bridge at the other end of the grassy knoll is the West Side Highway hugging Manhattan

Island from one end to the other. Although only one of my friend's families has a car, cars are still very important in our lives. From the *World Book Encyclopedia* at the Kingsbridge Library I carefully try to sketch in my school notebook copies of diagrams of the inside workings of a car engine. It's hard to believe a liquid like gasoline explodes over and over inside an engine and doesn't blow up the whole car. Sparks from spark plugs light the gasoline inside a steel chamber and little explosions force pistons up and down turning a long shaft that then rotates the rear wheels. A magnificent invention. We all hope to buy a car the day we're seventeen.

It's easy to recognize the cars passing us on the West Side Highway. No cars have been made since America declared war. Most we see are from the nineteen thirties, a few from the twenties. The object of our *Car Competition Game* is to name the car as it approaches. When it passes, the insignias tell if we identified the car correctly.

"Here comes a 1940 Nash convertible coupe," Ray says. "I hope it has white sidewall tires."

"You're right, except it doesn't have white walls."

"Here's a contest winner, the 1939 Packard," Danny says. "A Gallup survey named it the most beautiful car in America."

"Wrong," Tom says. "It's the look-a-like '39 Oldsmobile."

"Here comes my favorite," I say. "The Hudson Six cruising alongside the Hudson River." I got it right.

"This is a 1932 Ford V-8, almost as old as we are," Tom laughs.

"I'll never afford a luxury car," Danny says. "This is the car I'll buy. The 1939 Plymouth sold then for $645. I've got six dollars and forty five cents saved so far."

I've been at the Hayden Planetarium a few times, and learned about stars and planets seeing them projected and moving across the planetarium's huge dome. At night a good place to look for falling stars is near the George Washington Bridge. Over the Hudson River between New York and New Jersey is a vast dark space away from city lights.

"Heaven is the bright and shining place on the other side of the firmament," I say. "God punched millions of small holes in the darkness to give us stars and also to tease us. I'm sure heaven's on the other side. Right now we're seeing light beaming down from heaven."

"We all know you've been to the planetarium, so don't pull this firmament crap on us," Tom says.

"It's a planetarium word alright. All it means is a vaulting sky and that's what we're staring at."

"I'll buy *O'Flynn's Theory of Heaven,* if you accept mine about hell," Danny says. "There's the red planet Mars up there. It flashes red light down on us. I think it's where the devil lives. Hell. And the red we see is from the roaring fire and oceans of blood."

"I think you're both right," Ray says. "If heaven's on the other side of the darkness, it has to be a huge place because almost everyone goes there. Mars is very small, we can hardly see it. This makes sense to me because I believe few people are evil enough to end up in hell. The nuns are not teaching us hell is on Mars, but I could believe it. I just can't believe one mortal sin sends you to Mars for all eternity."

"I'll accept *Daniel Brennan's Theory of Hell,* if you all accept my theory of heaven," I say. "I just hope no one wants to figure where in that dark arch above us are purgatory and limbo."

A full August moon like a juicy peach rises over the Palisades creating a bridge of warm light across the Hudson.

"Stretching out here by the George Washington Bridge on a beautiful summer night turns us into theologians, philosophers, and plain old weirdoes," Tom laughs.

"Philosophy is way over my twelve year old head," Ray says. "Let's get our feet back on this earth and walk over to those hungry girls from Washington Heights who are flirting with us. No more theories, just some Catholic action."

THE SULLIVANS IN Flushing are one of the few relatives who own a car, a dark blue 1939 Studebaker Commander Sedan with Automatic Hill Holder. Jack Sullivan told me his car was designed by Raymond Loewy the famous industrial designer who helped develop the World of Tomorrow theme for the 1939 World's Fair.

"You were impressed by the Steam Locomotive 6100 at the Fair," Uncle Jack recalls.

"I remember. It was the sleek black and chrome beauty that was running sixty miles an hour while standing still. My father told me there were rollers underneath the track so the train couldn't lurch forward and run down Fairgoers."

"That steam locomotive was designed by Loewy too," Uncle Jack says. "He's one of the designers who launched the word *streamlined* into America's consciousness."

We call Jack, uncle, but he's really my father's third cousin. He sells insurance door to door in apartment buildings all over Queens. Uncle Jack lost the sight in one eye when an open Clorox bottle fell from a high cupboard.

Once every summer Uncle Jack takes the O'Flynn children to Jones Beach. "This keeps Séamus out of the Harlem for at least a day," he tells my parents. "He can swim in the pristine Atlantic Ocean, far out on Long Island."

I hang out the window waiting for the Studebaker to drive up Loring Place. Uncle Jack is coming from Queens over the Bronx Whitestone Bridge. His children are with him. We get into Uncle Jack's exceptional automobile and he drives back over the Whitestone Bridge, continues on to Long Island to Jones Beach. The ride goes quickly because of Uncle Jack's song sheets. We sing his favorite song a few times...

I tell you every street's a boulevard in old New York
Every street's a highway of your dreams
It's a thrill to shop on 34th Street
And down on Union Square we like the people you meet
On Mulberry Street, have you ever been there?

Here's Uncle Jack and five ragamuffins singing our hearts out as we cruise along Meadowbook State Parkway to Jones Beach...

Every street's a boulevard in old New York
So keep smiling and you'll never wear a frown
Just remember there's an East Side
And an and Uptown and Down
That's why we're proud to be part of New York Town

After a day with five children at the ocean, Uncle Jack heads back to the city. We sing another of his favorite songs...

Oh Danny Boy, the pipes, the pipes are calling
From glen to glen, and down the mountainside

The summer's gone, and all the roses falling
It's you, it's you, must go and I must bide

Uncle Jack tells us *Danny Boy* is one of millions of young men who had to leave Ireland to find work in America, particularly during the Great Potato Famine of 1845-1850. Bagpipers pass through villages sending shrill toned melodies into the glens and mountains telling the young men the ships are waiting to take them across the sea. Danny's sweetheart sings of her love and grief...

But come ye back when summer's in the meadow
Or when the valley's hushed and white with snow
And I'll be here in sunshine or in shadow
Oh Danny Boy, Oh Danny Boy, I love you so.

THE CATHOLIC CHURCH is mysterious. There's no proof the religion being taught in school and reinforced at home, is true. When you press your nun-teacher for specific answers, she says you must believe on faith alone.

"Just because you can't see something doesn't mean it doesn't exist," my father says. "Remember when you put your wet finger into the lamp socket."

I know the Blessed Mother has appeared to Bernadette at Lourdes in France, and to peasant children in Fatima, Portugal.

She also appeared to Juan Diego as Our Lady of Guadeloupe in Mexico City. Now she's appearing in the Bronx. *The New York Daily Mirror* christened her the *Madonna of the Grand Concourse.*

Tony Scarpullo, a twelve-year-old boy like me, says the Blessed Virgin Mary appears to him in a small vacant lot on the Grand Concourse, a wide beautiful boulevard running the length of the Bronx. Most Jews in the Bronx live in the fashionable apartments on either side of the Grand Concourse. It's ironic. The Blessed Mother is visiting a lot in the most Jewish part of the Bronx. But then I reasoned, Jesus was a Jew, his parents were Jewish. Why not the Grand Concourse?

I smile when my parents say they're taking us to see the Madonna who appears every Thursday. My mother tells me to wipe that smile off my face. The church in Rome officially recognizes the Blessed Mother has appeared in Mexico, France and Portugal. Why not now in the United States? We have the largest Catholic population in the world. My mother thinks she must have a special message for us since we are in the middle of a world war.

"Speaking of heavenly messages, when is the pope going to open the last letter from the girl who saw the Virgin at Fatima," I ask as we stroll along the Grand Concourse.

"I read about it recently in the *New York Catholic News*," my mother says. "The letter was written after the Virgin appeared in 1917. It won't be opened until 1960. The letter contains the last message the Blessed Mother gave to the little girl."

"What do you think is in the letter?" I ask.

"It's probably something about the end of the world," my father says.

"I think it has something to do with peace. Peace on earth," my mother says.

"Have *holy letters* been delivered to the Grand Concourse?" my sister Siobhan asks.

"For heaven's sake, Siobhan," my father scolds. "Are you making fun of God?"

Police divert traffic. Rubberneckers and would-be-worshippers swarm over the hallowed site. I always enjoy seeing a full moon, but tonight it takes on an uncomfortable eeriness. On the makeshift altar is a statue of the Blessed Mother smothered in floral offerings. The lot is lighted by emergency generators. Candles can be purchased for ten cents. A solitary *prie-dieu* faces the altar. Tony Scarpullo kneels here every Thursday waiting for the Virgin's appearance.

Mrs Daly tells us she visited his apartment last Thursday. "Let's go to Tony's apartment," I implore.

I know my mother has an aversion to anything Italian. Yet the Mother of God has selected an Italian immigrant family for her first visit to the United States.

"Interesting the Blessed Mother didn't appear to an immigrant Irish family," I tease.

"There's no proof she comes here," my mother snaps. "There has been no comment from Cardinal Spellman on this apparition."

A policeman stands at the entrance to the apartment building. Scarpullo, 5E. It's a walk-up like ours.

A cardboard box is propped up by the Scarpullo's door. A sign says offerings deposited here are to be used to replace the carpet that is wearing out because so many visitors are touring the apartment. My father drops in a few coins.

A Franciscan priest in a hooded brown cassock greets us. "I'm Father Mario Micali, pastor of St Anthony of Padua Church."

"We're the O'Flynns from St Nick's."

"Welcome to the home of the Scarpullo family. Please don't touch anything in the apartment. You may walk through quickly, single file, turn around in the living room and then come out this same door. God bless you."

The apartment is spartan like ours. In the hallway hang five small portraits of the Virgins of Fatima, Mexico City and Lourdes, Pope Pius XII, and Cardinal Spellman of New York. The Scarpullos and their children are sitting on the living room couch quietly praying the rosary. Tony sits in a wing chair by a fake fireplace with a revolving aluminum log under lit with a red light. He holds a long rope rosary like the Franciscans drape from their belts. His eyes are almost closed, his lips mumble a Hail Mary or some other prayer. The Scarpullos look like marble statues. Perhaps this is where the apparitions take place. No, newspapers say the visions are in the vacant lot. If Tony does see the Blessed Mother, shouldn't he be happy and smiling? Still, I had a feeling something had happened to Tony.

When we squeeze our way out of the Scarpullos, the line to the fifth floor now stretches all the way down five flights. People who live in the building look surly. They have difficultly entering and leaving their apartments. Their lives have been disrupted the past few weeks. I notice the list of tenants in the lobby. Mostly Italian names, a few Irish and German. Probably most are Catholics. They may be irritable but I doubt they'll register complaints with the building's owners. After all, their pastor is practically living in the building. And, suppose Tony's telling the truth? He could end up a saint, or something. He could put in a few good words for his neighbors. They may make a movie of his life. Build a cathedral on this vacant lot on the Grand Concourse.

The evening cools down. Thick low clouds start to move from east to west. The moon is gone now. The lot is no longer vacant. Thousands of people stand quietly waiting for the visionary to come out of his apartment. They clasp rosary beads in one hand and lighted candles in the other.

Father Micali leads the procession carrying a gold monstrance with a communion host encased behind glass. Another priest carries an *asperger*, sprinkling holy water on everyone he passes, then Tony wearing the rope rosary around his neck, then the Scarpullos.

The entourage files into the front row. Tony kneels alone on the *prie-dieu*. Father Micali begins praying the rosary.

"We'll begin with the Joyful Mysteries. The first Joyful Mystery is the Annunciation, when the angel announced to the Virgin Mary she was to be the mother of Jesus. Hail Mary full of grace..."

No one can see Tony's face. He's staring intently at the altar. The clamor of the Grand Concourse rises when there's a pause in prayers. The IRT Elevated clanks along two blocks away. We're now onto the Sorrowful Mysteries.

"The first Sorrowful Mystery," Father Micali says, "is the Agony of Our Lord Jesus Christ in the Garden of Gethsemane. Hail Mary....."

Tony's head suddenly lurches back. His parents hold Tony's shoulders.

"...Blessed are thou among women, and blessed is the fruit of thy womb, Jesus..."

Tony is as stiff as a clerical collar. The crowd murmurs. Someone gasps. A piercing cry.

The charcoal mist above begins to dissolve. Luminous silver slivers cut through. All eyes look up at the brightening sky. The full moon bursts through the clouds. Moans. Cries. Sobbing.

"Dominus Vobiscum."

"Notre Dame."

"She's here," my mother gasps.

"Tony sees her," my father whispers. "His eyes are riveted."

"I don't see anything," I say.

"You're not supposed to see her," my mother snaps. "Only Tony sees her. Like Saint Bernadette at Lourdes."

The crowd falls to their knees on damp weeds. Newspaper reporters move closer. Cameras flash.

"It's a miracle."

"...Glory be to the Father and the Son and the Holy Ghost," Father Micali continues praying the rosary.

Tony kneels ramrod for a few minutes. He's staring above the altar. Suddenly, his head falls forward into his hands.

"Is she gone?" my sister Sinead asks.

"I think so," my father says.

"Isn't it strange the moon popped out like that," I say. "I'm scared."

"There's nothing to be scared about," my mother says.

Tony writes a few lines on a pad. He hands it to Father Micali.

"Thank you for coming this evening," Father Micali says. "The Madonna did visit Tony again. Her message this evening is "Dear Children, I beg you to continue praying the rosary. The world needs prayer. Let nothing block your way to holiness. Let your own light shine. Prayer will bring peace to this war torn world." The Scarpullos start to leave the lot. We walk behind them. Mr Scarpullo says they will not open their apartment to visits until next Thursday.

"Can I touch Tony?" someone asks.

"Can I ask Tony to pray for my son?"

"I'm sorry," Mr Scarpullo says. "We're tired."

Walking home I ask my parents if they believe the Virgin Mary came to the Grand Concourse.

"Something extraordinary happened tonight," my mother says. "Many people were moved in a special way. Maybe it will help all of us develop a stronger prayer life. You couldn't have seen Tony praying and not be touched."

My father says: "That vacant lot became a sacred space. Grace was flowing like the Hudson River along the Grand Concourse."

TWENTY-TWO

President Truman in his radio address says "The flags of freedom fly all over Europe today."

The day before, the German high command signed an unconditional surrender ending the war in Europe.

At noon on May 8 the nuns take the entire school to St Nick's for a Victory mass. Our parents are there, standing room only. But there is no jubilation. Father Kruger offers prayers of thanksgiving for the cessation of hostilities in Europe. But the war with Japan in the South Pacific is still raging.

"Thank the Lord," my mother says. "It's Victory in Europe Day."

Father Kruger closed the school. The alleyway is clattering with radio commentaries and ringing telephones. Someone is banging a pot. I look out my bedroom window. It's my father. He's hanging out the kitchen window hitting our stew pot with a soup ladle just as he does every New Year's eve. Danny tosses a roll of toilet paper off the roof. The tissue streams down five stories bouncing off a car below. Within minutes roofs are covered with launches of toilet paper streamers. I climb onto our fire escape and yell across the street to Brendan McGinty to go out on his fifth floor fire escape and try to catch my roll. It works. He throws it back and then we both go down to the fourth floor and try again. Soon there's a tissue bridge connecting every fire escape. Sacks of paper confetti come out windows. Loring Place looks as beautiful as it does during a heavy snowfall. Except this is May and the sun is warm.

Everyone is giddy. I ring all twenty bells in the entrance of 222 knowing this is one time I will not get into trouble. Apartment doors are open and neighbors hug each other. Confetti floats down the stairwell. Voices and laughter grow louder. On Fordham Road trucks and cars toot horns and trolleys *clangclang.* Police cars and ambulances sound sirens. I hear the horns of the New York Central and elevated subways. Shrill blasts from boats on the Harlem River. Chimes of St Nick's are playing Gounod's *Ave Maria.* Bells of nearby churches toll. Mayor LaGuardia announces air raid sirens in New York can be blasted all day.

The next day Sister Joan Marie tells me to go to the principal's office. I've received her summons only a few times in my eight years at St Nick's. It means trouble. I put on my repentant demeanor and walk into Sister's office with my eyes cast down. I didn't want to meet her gaze right off. She has a way of looking at you that makes your knees weak.

"Séamus, you know each year at graduation the Dominican Sisters select a boy and girl from the eighth grade to give the valedictory and salutatory addresses," Sister Catherine says. "We met last night to select the two students who will represent the class of 1945. Mary Reilly will be salutorian and you had the most votes to be the valedictorian. So, Séamus you'll be valedictorian next month." Sister Catherine says.

I think I cannot turn this down. "What's a *val-ah-dick-tore-e-an,"* I stumble.

"It's the person who says the last words on graduation day on behalf of all the eighth graders. You'll have to read two typewritten pages with great feeling. All the sisters think you can do it. I'll write the valedictory speech. You can add your own thoughts, with my approval of course. Your parents will be very proud of you."

I wasn't really being asked if I wanted to give the farewell speech. I was told I had to do it. I felt guilty remembering my recent entry into the Mortal Sinners Club.

"I'll be nervous if I have to get up in the pulpit in that huge church," I say. "Father Kruger and the other Augustinians are the only ones allowed up there. Even sisters like you can't go on the altar."

"Although women can't go on the altar, the church does make some exceptions. Mary Reilly will be allowed in the pulpit to give her address. This year will go down as one of the most historic and significant for our nation. Yesterday the free world celebrated. There's wide speculation Japan will give up in the next few months. Everyone will be in a celebratory mood. This could be the most wonderful and happiest graduation at St Nicholas since the armistice in 1918 ending World War I."

"Were you teaching here then, Sister?" I ask. It's difficult to tell a nun's age because only a few inches of face and two hands are exposed.

"No Séamus," she rockets back. "It's true I was here, but I was a student in the seventh grade."

I ran home. My mother is leaning over the tub wringing out sheets. She's never heard of a valedictorian either. She grabs me with soapy arms. "It's a great honor for all the O'Flynns. Just think. You'll be up in the pulpit giving a speech like Father Kruger."

"Now mom," I protest. "Don't go comparing me with one of the priests who do this every Sunday. I'm not certain I can get up there in a packed church. I could open my mouth and nothing will come out."

I'VE NEVER HAD my hair cut by a barber. A red and white spiral turns around inside a cylinder of glass at Salerno's

Barber Shop on the Grand Concourse. I wish I could go inside at least this one time for a haircut for my graduation next month.

My father has been my barber for thirteen years. I'm certain the word *barber* is a derivative of *barbarian*. He's mean when he gives me a haircut. I'm not in the best mood either. I dread this monthly ritual.

My mother bought two pieces of blue and white striped cotton just like barbers use. My father places one cloth on the bathroom tile floor, puts a stool on top and then wraps the other around my neck. For years no matter how hard my father tried, I still got prickly short hairs stuck in my shirt collars. I'm itching for hours. He thought he came up with a good solution. Before he gave me the last haircut he told me to strip down to my underpants. But hairs got in there too. I scratched my rear end for the rest of the day.

"Just a quick trim dad," I plead. "In a month I'm going to be in the pulpit giving the valedictorian address."

"Séamus, I can give you another haircut a few days before graduation."

"Dad, today's haircut *is* for graduation." I hoped all his mistakes would be grown out by then.

He walks around me saying *"Hhhuuummm."*

I liked it better when he just combed my bangs forward, placed a bowl on my head and used a scissors. But that's long ago.

"Don't move."

"I'm as stiff as the statues in the Hall of Fame at N.Y.U."

"You might lose part of your ear if you jerk like that."

"*Ooouccbh.* You did it again. You said you'd be careful."

"Did what, Séamus?"

"You didn't release the hand clipper all the way before you pulled it off my hair. You're just pulling out large chunks and the roots too." I get off the stool and point in the bathroom mirror. "Look, I've got a large bare spot where you just tore out the hair above my ear."

I tell my father he should buy one of those new electric hair clippers advertised in the Sears Roebuck catalogue. A Shick Hi-Speed Clipper is only two dollars and seventy-five cents. He's stubborn. He's used the hand clipper all these years and that's it. He isn't about to try something new.

"Think of the money we've saved by never going to the barbershop."

"You go. I don't."

"I have to go. Your mother doesn't know how to cut hair."

"Why not let me cut your hair sometime. I want revenge."

He inspects me like an Indian circling a covered wagon.

"Just a few more minutes."

When he yanks out clumps, he must cut the nearby hair shorter so there's a semblance of a match.

My father has two large hand mirrors so I can check his masterful haircut.

"Finished, Séamus. What do you think?"

I'm used to the hideous sight. I can see the clumps of hair torn out. A pink area represents his first mistakes an hour ago. Bright red welts are just a few minutes old.

Maybe my father is being influenced by G.I. crew cuts. I look like a lawn mower has run over my head from one ear to the other.

TWENTY-THREE

The western side of Sedgwick Avenue drops off suddenly creating The Woods, an area too steep to build more apartment buildings. The New York Central traverses the lower edge of The Woods, with the Harlem River a few feet from the railroad tracks.

The Woods is our Primeval Forest, a mystical place with no KEEP OFF THE GRASS signs.

We constructed a hideaway of brambles leaning on a lone gigantic moss covered boulder. In this clandestine setting we share deep dark secrets and smoke cigarettes. Freddie *liberated* his grandmother's battered emigration-from-Germany suitcase that we fill with items we don't dare keep in our dresser drawers. Danny's soldier brother brought back from Guam an English translation of the *Kama Sutra* with graphic photos of Indian statuary. A carton of SPUD MENTHOL COOLED Cigarettes. Tear sheets of the January 1942 *Esquire* magazine that has twelve luscious Varga Girls, one for each month. My favorite is Miss July, all legs and a see-through scanty white bathing suit:

MISS JULY, 1942

I'm patriotic each July
And put my curves on view
The men turned red - old maids turned white
And debutantes turned blue

We hear someone sliding down the path.

"Whose there?" Danny calls.

"It's me, Ray. There's a blue smoke screen hanging in the trees on Sedgwick Avenue. Someone's going to call the Fire Department."

We had each smoked about a dozen SPUDS. I tried to inhale a few times. The cigarette pack says the heat was taken out when the menthol is put in. But my throat hurts and my stomach's churning.

"Have you heard the news?" Ray asks. "President Roosevelt died an hour ago."

"It's impossible. We just saw him last summer. In the open car with Fala," I say.

"Wow," Danny says. "He's our leader. He's the only president I've ever had."

Quiet in The Woods is broken by the wheezing of the first commuter train steaming into the Fordham Road station.

"We'll probably remember this day, April 12, 1945, the rest of our lives," Freddie says. "Too bad it's a day we're getting dizzy on SPUDS."

IT'S ABOUT HER...*buttocks...red...welts...quivering....*

"Séamus, you've had it long enough. Pass it to Ray," Danny demands in a whisper.

"What's all the noise about, Séamus?" Sister Joan Marie, my eighth grade teacher, asks.

"Sorry, Sister. I just asked Danny something."

"There will be a written test in fifteen minutes on the sacraments," Sister Joan Marie says. "You're supposed to be studying. Please be quiet."

My face is as scarlet as Jill's welts. I thought I was daring when I hid Varga Girls in my dresser draw. This morning Jim McNamara brought *God's Little Acre* into the eighth grade classroom and is passing it around. He put large paper clips on both sides of the book so you can't turn the pages. He wants you to read what he has underlined in red. Then he turns around to watch your reaction.

"Why don't you let us read the book after school?" Ray asks Jim.

"This is a graduation treat from me to all of you," Jim tells us. "My brother was on furlough last week and left this copy under his bed. I'm going to let you read a few lines every day this week during our religion lesson, right under Sister's nose. Besides the girls in our class will wonder what we're reading. I'm not forcing any of you. You can choose to read it, or not. Only Garlic Breath Tony Esposito stuck up his nose. We all wonder about him anyway."

Jim told us when the book was published in 1934 the New York Society for Suppression of Vice brought an obscenity charge. The case was dismissed when the judge declared it was not pornographic. I guess real pornography must be shocking if what I read this morning isn't considered bawdy.

She has...*a pair of rising beauties...*

Why would Erskine Caldwell give his book the title *God's Little Acre?* Why would he bring God into such risqué writing?

Yet, I can't wait to read tomorrow's selection.

Walking home, Danny says "Have you heard about the Catholic girl who is doing it on a date and the guy says breathlessly, Kiss me. And the Catholic girl says, no way. I shouldn't even be doing *this*."

"That tired old joke came to you after reading today's installment of *God's Little Acre*. Right?"

"Of course, Séamus. It certainly gets you thinking about a lot of things."

"What I've heard is when a husband and wife do it, the feeling they get is as close to heaven as you can get in this world."

"The worst joke I've heard," Ray says, "is about the woman whose husband dies and goes to the doctor for a physical. She has on a brightly colored dress, a pink silk slip, pink bra and black panties. The doctor says, 'You seem to have gotten over your husband's death quickly. You certainly look cheery. But how come you have black panties on? And she replies, 'That's where I miss him the most.' "

"Filthy piiggg." I say.

I THOUGH ABOUT Hedy Lamarr, the first actress to take all her clothes off in a movie. Danny and I were in Times

Square. We noticed a sign TENTH ANNIVERSARY DOUBLE FEATURE, Hedy Lamarr in *Ecstasy* and Fay Wray in *King Kong*. Both films were made in 1934 the same year as *God's Little Acre* was published. Because of the nude scene in *Ecstasy* we had to plead with grownups to take us into the theater, like we were their kids. Hedy Lamarr is splashing around in a milky pool. You can see she's not wearing a bathing suit. She steps out of the pond. There she is, all of her. Everyone in the country was talking about the scene and here I am seeing the famous Miss Lamarr with my own eyes. I was disillusioned when I later learned she was wearing a skin colored leotard. King Kong, on top of the Empire State Building, grasps Fay Wray. Her blouse opens and one breast is partially exposed. The ape is smitten. We must have been too. Stayed to watch both movies again.

The next day instead of *God's Little Acre*, we passed around our graduation Autograph Books.

TWENTY-FOUR

The opening page of our graduation autograph book admonishes us eighth graders...

Many years hence, whenever
I shall look at this album
I shall think of you.

So my dear friends, think of what you write:

"Your words must not only be clever,
"But fit to adorn this book forever."

LIST YOUR FAVORITE:

AUTHOR.................. *Washington Irving*
BOOK .... *Legend of Sleepy Hollow*

SONG........................ *Bell Bottom Trousers*
SPORT...................... *Stick Ball and Swimming*
HERO........................ *Colin Kelly*
PROFESSION......... *Writer and Author*
MOTTO.................... *Do unto others as you would have them do unto you*

Before moving to Long Island, Joan wrote....

May 30, 1945

Dear Séamus,
If I were a head of cabbage
I'd cut myself in two
I'd give a leaf to everyone
But I'd give my heart to YOU
Yours till Bear Mountain Gets dressed
Joan - *P.S. Please write to me Séamus*

Best of luck & happiness always,
Love,
Mom

To Séamus:
Good luck and Best of Wishes
in your school years to come to
a swell son
From Pop

God Bless You, Séamus
Sister Joan Marie

Séamus is a very good boy
He goes to Church on Sunday
He prays to God to give him grace
To flirt with the girls on Monday

Yours till the Statue of Liberty sits down
Jack Parker

I always did like you,
I never knew why
Maybe it's because you're
So handsome and shy!
Muriel Ann Camellia

Roses are red
Violets are blue
Sugar is rationed
Why aren't you?
Eileen Kelleher

First comes high school
Then comes college
Then comes Séamus
With a baby carriage

Yours till the Smith Brothers shave
Marty Meany

You asked me to write in your album
To put something original in
But there's nothing original in me
But the guilt of Original Sin
Uncle Gregory, U.S. Army

When you get married
And have twenty-five
Don't call it a family
Call it a tribe

Yours till Pepsi has 13 ounces
Ray Fitzgerald

Twinkle Twinkle Little Star
Séamus on the back of a trolley car
When the trolley goes off the track
Séamus puts the pulley back

Yours till Hitler sings God Bless America
and
Stay off the backs of trolleys, Séamus
Larry Nolan

Tables are round
Chairs are square
You and Joan O'Rourke
Will make a good pair

Yours till Palm Springs
Joe Brewster

When your wife
Hits you with a plate
Just think of
Your loving classmate
Joe McCormack

A girl is a friend
When she knows
All about you
But likes you

MY HEART PANTS 4 U
Mary Reilly

When we are old
And far apart
Whisper my name
to the Sacred Heart
Gerry Mawn

On this leaf in memory prest
May my name forever rest
Yours till Joe McCormack can
swim across the Harlem River
Jack McCabe

Being no poet
Having no fame
Permit me only
To sign my name

Yours till the devil goes ice skating
Ronald McLaughlin

Take a local subway
Change for an express
Don't get off
Till you reach success

Yours till I.D.K.
Babs Burns

I'd like to write your name in gold
But ink is all this pen will hold

Yours till the sidewalk talks
Dolores Galloway

Down by the river
Carved on a rock
Are three little words
"Forget me not"

Yours till Catskill Mountains
Ann Corrigan

When out on a meadow
Under a tree
Look at the nuts
And remember me

Your sister grad-u-8
Mary Galligan

Remember Grant
Remember Lee
The heck with them
Remember me
Kay Healey

There are big ships
There are little ships,
But the best ship is
"Friendship"
Anne Johnston

Don't make love
By the garden gate
Love is blind
But the neighbors ain't
Bobby Jennings

If in heaven we don't meet
Hand in hand we'll bear the heat
Dottie Hussey

Open the gate
Close the gate,
Here comes Séamus
the grad-u-8
Theresa Sinclair

Can't write
Bad pen,
Best wishes
Amen

Yours till Niagara Falls
Danny Moylan

U R
2 nice
2 B
4 gotten
Helen Day

Don't make love in a stable
Because the horses carry tails
Tommy Farrell

If by chance
this book should roam
Give it a kick
and send it home
Your sister Siobhan

You may fall from a rooftop
You may fall from the sky above
But the biggest fall you will ever have
Is when you fall in love
Sissy Coyle

Two in a hammock
With lips so tightly pressed
Pop gave the signal
And the bulldog did the rest
Kay

When you get married
And have a flat
Send me a picture
Of your first little brat
Danny Brennan

Séamus is a buttercup
Séamus is a daisy
Séamus is the little boy
Who drives the girls all crazy

Yours till I hate Van Johnson
Maureen Brackin

Roses are red
Violets are blue
So is your mother

When the rent is due
John Curran

Congratulations and best of luck
for high school and always
Love from your sister Sinead

Dot
Blot
Forget me not
Eddie Sawyer

Black is for Harvard
White is for Yale
I hope you'll never
Wear these colors in jail
Margaret Connolly

Work a little, sing a little
Whistle and be gay
Read a little, play a little
Busy every day
Talk a little, laugh a little
Don't forget to pray
Be a bit of merry sunshine
All the Blessed Day

Yours till fish use umbrellas
Billie Christie

Friends are like melons
Shall I tell you why?
To find a good one
You must a hundred try
Joan Wirth

Remember the Bronx
Remember Brooklyn
Remember the girl
Who called you good lookin'
Marty Casey

When you are in the bathtub
Think of me with every rub
Tom Knight, The Class Poet

Be sure you play
with the tails on sentences
and not with the tails
on horses
Marty Finn

Brain numb
Can't think
Inspiration won't come
Bad pen
Bad ink
Poor poem
Worse poet

Best Wishes
Amen

Yours till boardswalk
Alice Mayhew

May your joys be as deep
as the ocean
and your sorrows
as light as the foam
Gini Frey

When you are married
and have nine
Don't stop
You're doing fine
Jim McNamara

When you are old
And ready to die
Call me up and I'll say
"Good Bye"
Mary O'Connor

Written on the inside back cover of my memory album:

June 12, 1945

Temperature 78

Humidity Dense
Some have written before me
and written nicely too,
BUT those who write
after me
will have to write on glue

Your fellow cell-mate
Eddy Flood

TWENTY-FIVE

EVERY DAY I practice the speech Sister Catherine has written for me.

As we pause on the first crossroad on the highway of life....

I'm surprised to learn I'm traveling down something as serious as the *highway of life*. Scary. I'm also approaching *a first crossroad*. Sister Catherine has laid some heavy stuff on me.

Last week, the eighth grade boys made a Spiritual Retreat preparing for graduation. For two days, Father Kruger kept pointing his finger at us saying how much we need Truth and Purity in our lives. He said we're about to take a major step into manhood. He gave us a Holy Card with a photo of St Nicholas School on the front saying Class of 1945. On the back is a biblical quote...

When I was a child
I used to talk as a child,
think as a child,

reason as a child;
when I became a man,
I put aside childish things.

HERE'S MY NAME in the graduation program. The ceremony begins with *Wagner's Processional...Star Spangled Banner...Ave Maria...*Mary Reilly delivering the Salutary address...Séamus William Patrick O'Flynn, Valedictorian... *Sweet Savior Bless Us E're We Go...*Solemn Benediction of the Blessed Sacrament...*Verdi's Recessional.*

I'm only thirteen and here I'm on a program with Wagner and Verdi. I begin to shake. Suppose I mess up the speech I've so diligently practiced for weeks.

As I walk up the aisle past my father, he grabs my arm and whispers, "You'll do fine."

I didn't hear a word of Mary's address. The applause means it's time for me to go up to the altar. From the pulpit I see my whole family filling a pew. My mother and father, Siobhan fifteen, Sinead eleven, Mary Rita, three, and my baby brother Mickey fifteen months, First Sergeant Gregory O'Leary and his new wife Nora. I can tell my mother is worried, but I see my father is smiling.

"Reverend Father Kruger, Reverend Fathers, Devoted Religious, Loving Parents and Kind Friends:

"Tonight, the class of 1945 comes to bid farewell to our Alma Mater. For many watchful years we have looked forward to this solemn and important moment and now it finds its happy realization in our graduation from St Nicholas Elementary School. As we pause on the first crossroad on the highway of life, we become aware of the efforts of those who have made graduation possible."

I never thought I'd be in a pulpit giving a speech. While Sister Catherine has been coaching me after school I've thought a lot about my brief thirteen years in New York. My journey to this crossroad has shown me mostly flashes of good, but there are a few snakes in the grass like Father Cronin, the Sweeneys, Mr McCarthy, the bully Johnny Christie, Hitler, Nazis, Mussolini and the Japs.

"To you, our dear parents, we are most grateful for your loving interest, relentless energy and noble self-sacrifice that have made a Catholic education a possibility for each one of us. Throughout these eight years, you have watched us grow in the ways of God and man. Your careful guidance during these vital years of our young lives will reap fruit a hundred fold in the future. Without your foresight, dear parents, such prospects would never be realized."

I never think much about my parents. They're just always around. They're smiling at me. My mother certainly tries to mold me. She's always harping about by impatience. I love to see her warm smile when I come home from school. I'm proud of my hard working father too. He never complains much, just keeps plugging away.

"To our beloved pastor, Reverend Father Kruger and his devoted priests, we are deeply indebted for their inspiring spiritual instructions, fatherly counsels and encouragement. We will ever be mindful of their keen interest in our spiritual and temporal needs."

Last year Father Kruger was gone for a month. The head of the Augustinians convinced him to go to a retreat center for priests with drinking problems. At mass we now serve him wine without alcohol, the kind of wine my mother says was around when Jesus lived. He's not throwing metal chairs at referees anymore. Neither are we. He puts his arm around me; he's like my second father. I know I'm not going to be a priest. Maybe my baby brother Mickey will be the first priest in our family. I want to be well educated like the Augustinians, to go on to college some day. I know my parents can't afford it, but I'll work it out somehow.

"To our kind teachers, the Sisters of St Dominic, we convey our sincere appreciation for their perseverance and patience with us throughout the years."

When Sister Catherine wrote the draft of my speech, she hadn't included anything about the Dominican Nuns. I told my mother I wanted to let them know how much our class appreciates them and she helped me write a few words of tribute. When I got my hand bashed by Sister Mary Ita, I guess I deserved it. Anyhow, the nuns at St Nick's are like extensions of my own mother, patient, kind and hard working.

"During our years at St Nicholas we have been made conscious of the beautiful virtues that should characterize our lives as ideal men and women. The cultivation of truth, charity, justice, purity, honesty and fidelity to duty are absolutely necessary for a happy and peaceful life."

It's a tall order to turn eighth-graders into ideal men and women. Truth and purity right now are two of the most elusive virtues. But most priests and nuns I've met are good role models. My parents are too. So are my uncles Gregory and Jack. I know the ten commandments by heart, but I don't live up to them. My father says it's a good idea to aim high, like for the top of the Empire State and if you only reach the sixty-third or seventy-first floor, you're doing just fine.

"The class of 1945 is going into a world that is bleeding because it has betrayed Truth. Men who betray truth betray themselves. We as graduates of a Catholic school must live truth. It must motivate every action of our daily lives. We cannot compromise when it comes to deciding right or wrong. We are equipped with a set of Catholic principles that are eternal and admit no change. We are living in an age in which fundamental truths of God and the Church have not only been attacked, but also rejected. We recognize the necessity of the return of mankind to these priceless principles if the peace of the world is to last."

Heavy stuff, especially about not compromising when it comes to right or wrong. Sometimes it's exciting to do something wrong. But later on, Catholic guilt clicks in. Maybe that's not so bad. Guilt becomes a waving red flag. Something's not o.k. Sister Catherine may be right when she wrote the worldwide rejection of basic truths is one of the main reasons we have been at war the past three and a half years.

"We further realize that Christianity is not a subject to be taught, but a life to be lived. Christ has taught us by His example the truths we are to believe and the means we must use to achieve peace and thus gain eternal life. He is the Way, the Truth and the Life. If we follow Him, we will not walk in darkness."

I look back to 1937 when I was in the first grade and realize how St Nick's influenced my life. I've been taught the same subjects as Everett Mendelsson who's in public school. But there's another dimension at St Nick's; we're also being educated in how we should live our lives. I don't understand all of it at this point. But I know I want to keep the peace I feel in my heart and soul on my graduation day.

"It is with these sentiments that we the class of '45 bids adieu to St Nicholas and march forward to become militant Catholics armed to defend the home front from the corrupting forces of atheism. Always shall we remain faithful to the beautiful and glorious ideals of our Alma Mater."

I've never met an atheist. I'm confused how they go about corrupting the home front. I don't feel militant either. In fact I feel just the opposite. A year ago, the O'Reillys in 1A at 222 lost their son Mark on the beaches of Normandy. Everyone walking along Loring Place sees the small memorial flag with a GOLD STAR in their living room window. I hate Germans and Japs. I'm glad the Germans surrendered last month and Hitler committed suicide. I hope he had stabbing pains after he drank cyanide. He didn't want to get caught so he made sure he would die by finally shooting himself in the head. We still have the Japs to beat. I'm not ready to turn the other cheek. I'm not totally faithful to the ideals of my Alma Mater. They're beautiful and glorious and worth thinking about, but I need some time right now.

FOR MY GRADUATION present I ask my parents to take the whole family to the top of the Empire State Building. My parents have lived in New York City for more than twenty years and have been to the top only the day I was christened. An excursion like this is expensive. The subway fare is a nickel. My mother no longer asks the three older O'Flynn children to sneak under the turnstile. My baby sister and brother ride free. Since I don't expect my parents to walk up 1,576 steps to the top, we need seven tickets. Cokes and cookies in the snack bar on the 86th floor add another few dollars. My mother figures my graduation present will be a little more than the five dollars they had decided to give me.

My mother has a right to hate elevators. Her brother Harry died when he was hit on the head by an elevator in the baggage room of Pennsylvania Station. She mentions his death as my father purchases the tickets. I said it was an accident. He shouldn't have looked up to see if the elevator was coming.

"Séamus he was killed twenty-two years ago. But I still see his body on the pallet they pulled out at the morgue. His handsomeness was crushed."

"Mom, this is a happy day," Siobhan says. "Nothing's going to happen. Uncle Harry was killed by a freight elevator. These are high speed passenger elevators."

"This pamphlet says there are sixty-three elevators," my father says. "Express to the top takes less than a minute."

"Suppose the cable breaks on the way down," my mother says.

"Even if it does," my father says calmly, "there's a giant spring at the bottom and we would just bounce up and down a bit."

"I'm doing this for you Séamus," my mother says entering the elevator cab with her eyes closed.

"Oh, no. Whooiieee," my mother shrieks as the elevator begins its ascent.

The operator says: "This is the world's tallest building. The site was purchased from the wealthy New York Astor family.

The old Waldorf Astoria Hotel was torn down so the Empire State could be constructed in 1931. It's twelve hundred and fifty feet to the tip of the mooring mast. It's covered with Indiana limestone and granite with strips of chrome-nickel steel. Ten million bricks cover the skin. There's enough floor space in here to shelter a city of eighty thousand people."

"There were only two thousand living in my little town of Skibbereen," my mother whispers to my father. She's relaxing.

The late afternoon sky is clear and the sun over New Jersey is flashing on the Hudson River. A brisk wind cools the summer day.

"Now I know why the Empire State is your favorite place in the whole city," my mother says. "This view is heavenly."

"It may be the closest to heaven we'll ever be," my father says.

A MONTH LATER, July 28, on a soupy-foggy Saturday morning, a B-25 bomber crashes into the 79th floor of the Empire State Building. I think of the times I've been on the observation deck on stormy days and wondrously swept my hands through rain clouds.

Danny and I take the subway to 34th Street. Pieces of the plane are strewn over the streets. We're able to get through to the loading dock and climb our secret stairs to the 79th floor. Firemen and hospital workers are everywhere. There's so much confusion no one asks why we're up here. Through a massive blowhole where the bomber hit, I see the hazy southern tip of Manhattan Island and the diminutive silhouette of the Statue of Liberty. The gasoline fire is out. I notice a large charred crucifix in the lobby of the burned out office. The bomber crashed into the office of Catholic War Relief Services incinerating ten of the agency's staff, plus three Air Force officers in the plane.

I recall my mother asking what would happen if an elevator cable broke. One of the B-25's engines crashed through the building into an elevator shaft and shattered a supporting beam. A twenty-year-old elevator operator, Betty Lou Oliver, was descending from the 79th floor when the cables were severed and the elevator plummeted. Special devices helped slow the fall but it slammed into a massive rubber bumper. Her back and legs were broken but she'll survive.

A week later, August 6, 1945, another bomber makes world news. *Enola Gay*, a B-29, drops *Little Boy,* the first atomic bomb used in warfare on the city of Hiroshima, killing over 80,000 people. A second atomic bomb, *Fat Man,* is dropped three days later on Nagasaki, killing 40,000.

On September 2, aboard the battleship Missouri, Japan signs an unconditional surrender, ending World War II.

CUMULUS CLOUDS TOWERING higher in the cool blue sky. Sun's moving south turning a golden corn color. When autumn comes, windows at 222 begin to close. Quiet at night in the alleyway. No longer need to cool off in the Harlem River. The World Series will start soon. The Yankees aren't going to make it. Looks like Detroit and Chicago.

I meet Danny at the nine o'clock mass and we agree it's time for a subway escape from the neighborhood. We catch the IRT elevated, pass the Yankee Stadium, change to the local at 125th Street and get off at 81st. When we first started going into Manhattan I noticed the new white brick apartment buildings with doormen on Lexington, Park and Fifth. My Uncle Gregory helped build some of the buildings on Fifth just before the Great Depression hit. Now I notice town houses on the side streets. Only three or four stories, not very wide. Black iron fences, gleaming doorknobs and knockers. Architectural filaments similar to the classical Greek and Roman friezes at the Metropolitan. White, pink and red inpatients in flower boxes at their September peak. Biting wind whipping down 78th Street. A limousine pulls into a circular drive at a splendiferous private club decamping a grande dame wrapped in fur.

The Metropolitan Museum's show of Greek treasures has been drawing crowds all summer. The prize is a 600 B.C. marble statue of a young man acquired by the Metropolitan in 1932. Kouros is almost six feet tall; his hair is braided and falls down to his shoulders.

"Greek artists imbued their statues with life's breath," the museum guide says. "No detail is missing. This is a magnificent example of an artist taking a lifeless piece of marble and painstakingly chiseling this living human being. The male nude like Kouros was the foremost subject of Greek artisans. This statue was probably commissioned by the state, which six hundred years before the birth of Christ, was the fountainhead of religious and political beliefs......"

I whisper to Danny: "The older I get the more I realize how little I know."

THE NEXT DAY I'm bounding down 222's five flights of stairs two at a time. "Good morning, boys. I'm Brother Patrick, the new principal," says the bald man in a black cassock. A silver cross hangs below a white starched dickey. My first day at St Nick's High School.

12317947R00159

Made in the USA
Lexington, KY
09 December 2011